An Excuse to Kill

Christopher Malinger

B̶P̶

An Excuse to Kill
By
Christopher Malinger © 2025

Cover design by Sean Malinger

Back cover copyright © Shutterstock 162262712 All rights reserved.

Polar Photography Publishing: Summerfield, FL 34491.

www.polarphotography.com

ISBN: 13: 9781736244685

ISBN: 10: 173624468X

To the Sisters of Notre Dame from Saint Stanislaus
Grade School
and
Notre Dame High School in Milwaukee, Wisconsin
who guided me for twelve years.
Thank You

Chapter One

Sam Jackson had settled into his hotel room when he heard a knock on his door. He wasn't expecting visitors and swung out of bed with some hesitation. He grabbed his long-sleeve shirt, using it as a makeshift robe, and went to the door.

The view from the eyepiece revealed an attractive redhead waiting for a response. Her scarlet hair, partially covered with a nondescript baseball cap, cascaded onto her shoulders. Beads of moisture highlighted her hair and fur collar, no doubt the result of the snowstorm. That concern about the weather convinced him to remain in his room rather than seek the diversions of Flagstaff's social life. Sam opened the door.

"Yes?" he asks, a little skeptical yet thinking it might be his lucky night.

She was tall and in her mid-thirties. Her green eyes were at eye level with Jackson's eyes, and they possessed a tempting quality that suggested his thoughts may be accurate. Her opened fur-lined ski jacket revealed ample breasts under a tight Flagstaff T-shirt, which could have served as a billboard for a traveler on Route 66. With one leg in a brace, she leaned on a crutch with the obvious intent to steady herself.

"I'm sorry to trouble you at this late hour, but I've locked myself out of my room. Could you call the front desk and ask them to come and unlock my door?" She nodded toward her crutch, adding, "It's difficult to get around--skiing accident. I'm just too tired for another trip to the lobby."

"Sure. What's the room number?"

Her one free gloved-hand motions to her right. "Room 309."

"Hang on, I'll give 'em a call," he says, with an infectious smile that would normally charm the pants off any female. He waves her in while she checks the door's swing, wedging her crutch between it and the jam.

With the speed of a rattler, she pulls out a Sig Sauer and fires two noise-suppressed rounds into Jackson's back.

He jackknifed forward, unable to break his fall. It would have made little difference, for he was dead before hitting the ground. Jackson, now motionless on the floor, while two crimson blotches spread around dual holes, staining his hastily donned shirt.

The night visitor closed the door, re-holstered the weapon inside her jacket, and coldly steps past Jackson's lifeless body.

Chapter Two

I have a confession to make. My reason for moving to Flagstaff is simple. I wanted to get away from the crime in New York City. The other reason, if you don't think that's enough, is my ex-wife. I won't bore you with the details, but the town just wasn't big enough for the two of us. Yeah, a city of over eight million people wasn't big enough for the two of us. I got the idea of moving from a billboard that showed this chick smiling with a beautiful snow-capped mountain in the background, and thinking I could do that. I envisioned myself skiing down the slope, enjoying a hot toddy, and meeting that babe in the picture as we chit-chatted around the fireplace in some ski lodge.

Anyway, that's what I thought, or maybe it was another part of my body doing the thinking. When I got this job, I was all gung-ho until I saw the ski hills up close and personal. The picture on the billboard didn't do them justice. I figured a person could get hurt—I mean, going down an icy slope without brakes, one could run into a tree. And about the crime—they have it over here, too, except the scenery is better. Somehow, I had this notion that any town west of the Mississippi was like Mayberry. Well, it's not. Route 66, or what's left of it, draws criminals and tourists, and tourists also commit crimes. Who would have thought?

My name is Jack Owens, and I work for the Flagstaff Criminal Investigations Division. My partner, Stanley Kowalski, is out making a donut run. And yeah, it's a *cliché*, but a guy is gotta eat, right? He had the same idea as I did, only he left Milwaukee about nine years ago. Honestly, the only things that I know that came out of that town are beer and a baseball team that wanted more money and a warmer climate.

My reason had something to do with a warmer climate, but those snow-capped mountains should have been a tipoff for me. Flagstaff gets cold, and it does snow—it just doesn't last as long.

When I applied for this job, I had to go through a background check, mental evaluation, and physical—check, check, and double-check. Unlike the first time I applied for a job in the NYPD using a paper questionnaire, I did the mental screening with a computer. The questions were like, what nimrod would pick the wrong option? "Why did you choose a career in law enforcement? A: I want to protect and serve, B: I need the money, C: I like to shoot people, and D: All of the above." I decline to make my answer public, but I passed.

While waiting for Kowalski to return with our breakfast, I walk over to the duty desk to check out the police blotter and see what has happened since yesterday. I spotted a couple of familiar names and the usual offenses, like drunk and disorderly. The trouble is it never stops there, eventually—it leads to the big stuff, and that's where I come in.

I spot Kowalski walking across the parking lot, shuffling his number twelve shoes through the few inches of snow we got overnight. He's a big guy, and his size is intimidating, which is good from my perspective. I call him my muscle. The trouble is, his heart is as sweet as the Danish he's most likely carrying in those little white bags nestled between the two coffee cups in the cardboard carrier. I head over to the office to meet him.

With an enormous smile, he says, "Mornin', Jack." He hands me a white bag. "Sorry, they didn't have the Danish, so I got you a cruller instead. I think the snow plow crews got there first."

"That's all right, that's the advantage of running a snowplow, yah get the first pick of the donuts."

Kowalski laughs. He set down the tray and slipped off his black overcoat. "You check out the blotter?"

"Yeah, same stuff, same creeps."

No sooner did I sit down when Officer Martinez pokes his head in the doorway and shouted, "Got a shooting for you guys at the Double Six Hotel."

"That's it?"

"Yeah. The manager reported it, and one of our patrol cars responded. That's all I know."

"No active shooter?"

"Nope," says Martinez before disappearing.

I took a large bite of my cruller before washing it down with some coffee.

"Whaddaya think?" asks Kowalski before giving me his professional opinion. "Suicide?"

"Won't be the first time some bozo gets a room to save their family the trouble of cleaning up the mess."

Kowalski licks his fingers and goes to get the overcoat he draped over his desk chair. "Owens, you coming?"

"Hey, give me a break. I just started my meal. Besides, if I see the body and it ain't pretty, I'll lose my appetite."

Kowalski ignores me and continues putting on his coat. The one thing that burns me about him is that he's always in a hurry. The other one thing is that he has a beautiful wife and kids, while I'm spending half my income on a woman over two thousand miles away who couldn't care less about me. Let's see, that's two, but I digress. I take a couple of big bites and a sip of coffee to ease the lump down my gullet.

"Okay, mother hen, let's go."

Chapter Three

The Double Six Hotel is one of those places that was called something else before assuming its third alias. This I knew from squad-room gossip. It went from a four-star to a two, but it wasn't what anyone would call a dive. Interestingly, this was my first visit. Any previous crimes in the place were cut-and-dry or handled by one of the other members of our unit or uniformed squad. I thought —it didn't have the sheen of a Hyatt—but few places do. When we approached the desk, the clerk was talking to a couple of guests. They appeared to be a couple of ordinary tourists who probably picked this hotel by mistake on their way to Albuquerque or Los Angeles.

We flashed our badges at the desk clerk, whose name tag says Tammy. She excused herself and turned around to open the door to the back room. "More policemen are here, Sharon."

The guests eyed each other before redirecting their attention to us.

I smile. They didn't.

Sharon comes out of her office, proceeds to a side door, and emerges around the corner into the lobby. She gives me a quizzical glance and reserves a smile for Kowalski while extending her hand in my direction. Maybe I still had sugar glaze from the cruller on my face?

"I'm Sharon Macfarlane, the hotel manager. I suppose you want to see the room?" she says in her inside voice, the voice a person uses when they don't want other guests to know there has been a murder in her hotel. She was matronly looking. Despite her obvious mid-thirties, her choice of tight-fitting clothing did little to hide her chubbiness, which I assume was the intent. When I see a babe like that, I sometimes wonder if they think the tightness of the clothing makes them look trimmer, but maybe I don't know women.

Taking her hand, I say, "I'm Detective Owens, and this is Detective Kowalski. Yes, please take us to the room."

"Pleased to meet you, but these circumstances can be less than pleasant," she says, her focus leaping from me to Kowalski.

What was I to say? This always makes my day. I grimaced and released my hand.

She turned and began leading us to the elevator. "Someone from your police department is already up there. They didn't seem interested in anything I said, only if anyone heard gunshots."

"And?" I ask.

She shook her head. "No, nothing at all. I'm not really surprised."

"Why's that?"

"The adjoining room was unoccupied, as well as the room across the hall. Besides, each room is soundproofed with cinderblock walls."

The elevator doors opened, and a young couple exited, guiding a luggage carrier. We stepped aside, allowing them to pass. The girl, maybe in her late twenties, gives me a smile, which I return.

We remained silent during the ride—everyone was more interested in the changing display of the floor numbers. Upon reaching the third floor, we follow Sharon to the room at the far end of the hallway. She uses her master key to open the door.

I turned to her and say, "Thank you, Sharon. We'll be down to see you when we're done. In the meantime, I would like you to print a list of all your guests. And one more thing, call the person who was on duty last night. We need to ask him or her some questions."

Sharon hesitated as we pushed our way in, impersonating a pigeon and bobbing her head back and forth to get a glimpse. Kowalski closes the door, ending the show for her.

An Excuse to Kill

Grayson Donelly, his back to us, turned when we entered. His partner, Emily Rugger, gave us a wave. The victim lay sprawled out on the floor with two small bullet holes on the left side of his back, bloodstaining his powder-blue shirt. Besides the murder, the ransacked room indicated this was a professional hit.

Chapter Four

D ouglas McGuire, just Doug to his friends, arrives at 10:45 a.m. The presence of several police vehicles in the parking lot sparks his curiosity. When he called for police help during his shift, a single car with uniformed cops usually responded. He uses his passkey to unlock the side entrance to the front office.

"Hi, Tammy. What's going on? Where's Sharon?"

"Hi, Doug. Sharon's in the kitchen making coffee. We had a murder on the third floor," Tammy Williams, the assistant manager, replies excitedly.

"Murder? When?

"The police figured during your shift. I tried to call you after the cleaning staff discovered the body."

"Yeah ... about that. I unplugged my phone. My ex-wife has been bugging me lately. She still thinks she deserves more money after the sale of the house–even though it was part of the divorce settlement. I'm just here to pick up my check. I gotta do some banking this morning."

"Well, the police will want to talk with you first. I told them you didn't start until later tonight."

He throws his backpack under the front counter and straightens his tie. With a hand on the door leading to the office, he pauses, turns to Tammy, and asks, "What room?"

"Room 301. The guy's name was Samuel Jackson. Do you remember him?"

The name not only sounded familiar, but he remembered the special request from him. He recalled checking him in shortly after starting his shift. Jackson asked if he could deposit a manila envelope into the hotel's safe. Normally, Doug would have refused, as the use of the safe by guests were strictly forbidden, but the tip of fifty dollars was too much of a temptation.

"Yeah, other than checking him in, that's about it."

"One more thing, you put an envelope in the hotel's safe with a paper-clipped note and your name on it," she says, her voice heavy with indictment.

Blushing at the charge, he fumbles a reply. "I-I was reviewing my car insurance. I didn't want it lying around when I made my rounds. I just forgot about it ... it won't happen again."

"You know the policy about the unauthorized use of the hotel's safe." She reaches under the counter, retrieves the offending envelope, and hands it to him. "Here, I pulled it out before Sharon saw it."

Snatching it from her waving hand, he says, "I know, I know, it won't happen again." Unsure what to do, he hesitates, then bends over to unzip his bag and slides the envelope in.

Tammy gives him a dismissive wave. "You better get going. They're in the office looking over the guest list from last night. I think the police are going to be happy you're here."

When Doug opens the door, two plainclothes detectives look up from the printouts on the desk. "Hello, I'm Douglas McGuire. My manager told me you wanted to talk with me."

Both detectives rise and reach out, taking turns shaking Doug's hand. They introduce themselves as Jack Owens and Stanley Kowalski. "Have a seat, Mr. McGuire. We need to ask you a few questions about last night," Inspector Owens says as he resumes sitting.

Inspector Kowalski, already sitting, retrieves a notebook from inside his suit coat pocket.

"I understand you were on duty when Mr. Jackson checked in. Was there anything unusual about him?" asks Owens.

"Unusual?"

"Yeah. Maybe he said something or did something noteworthy—you know, odd," Kowalski chimes in.

Knowing his use of the safe by a hotel guest could cost him his job, he shakes his head. "Nope. He came in around eleven, paid with a credit card, and asked what time breakfast was served. That's it. You can check the exact date and time from the computer." The palms of his hand sweat. "It was a pretty uneventful evening."

Without looking up, Kowalski continues to take notes and then asks, "Did any of the hotel's guests report any unusual sound or noise?"

"As I said, it was a pretty normal shift," Doug says, appearing to have another thought, adds, "Well, as far as I was concerned, anyway. My boss told me someone had killed Mr. Jackson. Can you tell me how he died?"

The detectives share a glance, and then Owens says, "He was shot. The medical examiner says it was between eleven and midnight. What were you doing around that time?"

"You don't think I killed him, do you?"

"Just answer the question," snaps Owens.

"Usually, around that time, the drunks start coming in. So, I stay close to the front desk. After three o'clock, I lock the front door."

"Did anyone call the desk and complain about the noise?" asks Kowalski.

Doug shakes his head. "Doesn't it seem odd that someone died during a robbery on the third floor? I mean, why go up several floors only to rob someone when you could do that on the first floor?"

Again, the detectives exchange looks. "We didn't say anything about a robbery, Mr. McGuire."

"I just assumed ... ."

"You some sort of amateur detective?" asks Owens.

Doug gave a dismissive wave. "I write mystery novels."

"Oh?" Owens smiles. "Have you sold any?"

"No," Doug confesses sheepishly.

"Well, maybe you need to do more research," mocks Kowalski.

Owens and Kowalski share a muted laugh while Doug turns a shade of pink.

"It's ... it's only a hobby. It helps pass the time. I'm hoping that someday I'll get published. Right now, I'm only trying to keep my head above water after going through a messy divorce."

Owens, his smile gone, nods. "What do you do during your shift, Mr. McGuire?"

Shifting, Doug rattled off his nightly tasks, rehearsed from previous accountings of his time with management. "Check-in and out guests, answer the phone, transfer calls, take reservations, do the night audit, clean up the front desk and office, and set up the breakfast bar."

"You can't have a lot of work after midnight?"

"All hell can break loose between midnight and three in the morning. Trust me. Working the graveyard shift, I sometimes wonder if my pay differential is worth it."

"I'm sure that may be the case," Owens agrees, "but that isn't every night. So, what do you do when things are quiet around here?"

"Well, between you and me," Doug begins, his voice lowered, "I write. You know, that's when I work on my novels. I use the office's Selectric typewriter, but I don't advertise that to my boss. It helps keep me awake. I'd appreciate it if you'd keep that between us."

Showing no interest in Doug's rambling confession, Owens reaches into his coat pocket. "We'll go through the hotel's security tapes, and we may contact you regarding our findings. In the meantime, if you think of anything, call us." He hands him a business card.

Doug accepts the card. "I will," he instinctively replies, in a tone long rehearsed in answer to hotel guests requesting a service.

Chapter Five

Doug McGuire always knew he was under the watchful eye of the surveillance camera. After years of its vigilant gaze, it became an accepted intrusion that one lives with as a condition of employment. Eventually, he ignored it—until now.

He waited late into his shift until he was certain the likelihood of being disturbed was remote. Doug retrieves the mysterious envelope from his backpack. Earlier, he thought of opening it in the privacy of his apartment. His reluctance was more out of caution about contacting the police without his employer knowing or losing his job. It was too much of a gamble, and his procrastination brought him to the present, whether to call Detective Owens or unseal the envelope. It was late, and certain the detective would be at home sleeping. He plays with the card before slipping it into his shirt pocket.

Sitting below the countertop, with only his head visible to the observant eye of the camera, he pulls down a newspaper off the counter. Pretending to read the news, he discreetly uses his pocketknife to slice open the envelope and remove its contents.

When Doug accepted the envelope, he told Mr. Jackson when he would go off duty. He became concerned when Jackson didn't contact him at the end of his shift and wondered if he shouldn't call his room to remind him.

Again, his procrastination caused him to forget about the envelope, a frequent flaw his ex-wife found necessary to remind him of.

Doug unfolds the trifold single sheet of paper with great curiosity, only to find a small envelope affixed to it. The only marking on the enclosure is the word Two Guns. No longer careful and now sure of the item's identity by touch, he impatiently rips off the transparent tape that secures the attachment. With a faint metallic clink, he lets the key fall onto his opened newspaper.

You didn't need to possess the skills of Sherlock Holmes to know the reason behind the death of the man in room 301. Still, in the grip of remorse for holding back on his account to the police, he realizes Lady Luck may have dealt him a winning hand. To kill for this key reinforced its importance.

Doug, in the throes of euphoria, figured the murder would ultimately fade. The police, unaware of the existence of this envelope, would eventually drop the case. Samuel Jackson's death was a robbery gone wrong. Yeah, he only has to wait it out.

The wall clock shows it is nearly three thirty. He stuffs the sheet and key back into the envelope. Something, previously unnoticed from the larger envelope, floats onto the floor. He leans over to retrieve it and discovers a matchbook cover. The matchbook shows wear, and the cover is from a now-defunct KOA campsite. He scans a neatly printed column of unrelated words and numbers on the inside flap: *pool steps-327.31º, lion-78.86º, bridge-31.60º.* In his mind, he realizes the matchbook is key to Jackson's death.

Realizing it is getting late, he puts everything on hold. Now, it is no longer a time for speculative fantasy. He needs to print the statements for people scheduled to leave before sliding them under their doors. After that, his morning tasks would include making coffee and prepping the breakfast nook for the food staff. Secretively, he slips the envelope inside the newspaper, turns away from the counter and into the office, and then slides it into his backpack.

He completes his duties with a flurry of efficiency, ready for the morning's onslaught of guests.

"Morning," Phyllis Logan greets as she enters through the side door of the clerk's counter.

Wrapping up the last duties of his shift, Doug looks up and acknowledges her arrival. "Mornin', Phyllis," he replies in a melodic tone. He likes her and even fantasizes about having a relationship with her. Unfortunately for his self-esteem, she ignores them and sometimes mocks his innocent flirtations with taunting laughter.

"How did it go last night? Any murders?" she jests with ghoulish amusement.

"No, not this time," he says, his high-pitched voice awkward with the resonance of a teenager.

Thinking her presence was the reason that made his voice squeak, she teasingly adjusted her blouse to reveal more cleavage. She catches him taking a peek and smiles.

Embarrassed, he cleared his throat and turned a shade of pink. "I'll sign off and be on my way. Tammy told me she would be in late. I guess she needed more sleep after dealing with the cops."

"That's okay. I can handle it," she says in her usual air of overconfidence.

As Doug was about to leave through the side door of the front office, a tall, middle-aged man approached the front desk. Dressed in a gray herringbone sport coat with black dress slacks, Doug thought his attire was insufficient for the cold weather.

Phyllis extends her rehearsed greeting. "Good morning, sir. How may I help you?"

Doug continues toward the exit.

"Yes, I am looking for Samuel Jackson. I'm running a little behind because of the snowstorm. I hope he hasn't checked out?"

Doug freezes. With his hand on the door, he glances over his shoulder and eyes the man with concern before pushing his way outside.

Chapter Six

Addicted to my New York diet of donuts, I wave a couple of white paper bags in the air toward Stan, much like Eve, who suckered Adam into giving up the garden. His face broke into a smile, like a Pavlovian dog's conditioned reaction. The glazed, filled-with-jam donuts weren't as good as Orwasher's Bakery on the Upper East Side, but as they say, "When in Rome ..." In my assessment, a lot of things in Flagstaff weren't as good as the shops and eateries of New York. Personally, I think Flagstaff needs more delis than cheap Route 66 souvenir crap.

"Morning, Stan. I thought I'd bring breakfast, considering the late night we had."

"Ya know, my wife thinks you're a bad influence."

"Funny she should say that because I hafta agree. So, you want me to keep both bags?"

"Mary has her opinions, and I have mine." Stan reaches out.

I say, "Good call," and hand him the bag.

I move to the coffeepot and pour my first cup. "In all my years on the NYPD, this case ranks high on the smell-o-meter."

Kowalski nods. "Yeah, a third-floor robbery, a phony name like Samuel Jackson, and a night clerk whose clammy handshake tells me he knows more than he's admitting. Besides all the evidence of a search by the killer, the big tipoff is why would a robber remove an ironing board cover? Obviously, he, or she, was looking for something flat."

"This isn't a robbery."

"So, you thinkin' what I'm thinkin'?" asks Kowalski.

"Yeah, it's a hit. Let's head down to the AV room and see what secrets we'll find in those tapes."

I grab my cup of joe, bagged breakfast, and move down the hall. As I walk into the AV room, I reach around the corner and flick on the light switch. The place was as cold as the parking lot. For a second, I thought I could see my breath as the banks of recessed fluorescent ceiling lights struggled to come alive.

"I don't know who the hell designed the heating system in this place, but they should be shot with shit," I say with my usual air of disdain.

"I think it was a low-bidder," Kowalski says while setting his repast and drink on the counter.

"Yeah, it always is." I place my coffee and bag on a nearby table.

The audiovisual room is small, no bigger than an efficiency apartment. Its interior, further crowded with electronic gear, looks as if it hadn't been cleaned in several weeks. Electrical and video cords lay coiled in bundles over the equipment or hung in loops on the walls. Two televisions sit on top of a gray industrial rack, which protrudes into the room, further adding to the claustrophobic feeling.

"Stan, bring that cart with the VHS player over here."

Kowalski unravels the feed cord attached to the television. Once the player is within reach, he plugs in the line. As the screen slowly brightens, we help ourselves to the contents of the bags.

"Two donuts?" says Kowalski, smiling at the discovery. I retrieve the hotel's security tape from the pocket of my overcoat. I insert the cartridge and take a seat next to Kowalski, who is eagerly consuming his first glazed donut.

With my free hand, I reach out and push the fast-forward button to about where I thought was the hour before the night clerk came on duty. With sporadic jerks, the tape advanced to Douglas McGuire's arrival at the front desk. "We'll start from here," I say before taking my first bit of my donut.

Alternating between sips of coffee, I advanced the tape to the time of Jackson's arrival. At that point, Kowalski says, "Let it run in real-time, Jack."

I push play, allowing the images to advance in real time. Without removing our eyes from the television, we mechanically down coffee while taking alternating bites from our breakfast. The dial on the wall clock jerks forward with each recycled scene.

Jackson arrives with a suitcase and briefcase. The luggage remains on the floor. Only once did he access the briefcase during check-in.

"What do you make of that, Stan?"

"Beats me. It looks like he's getting something from the bag."

The camera switches to the side entrance, lingers, then moves to the other side entrance before shifting to the vacant pool. When it returns to the front desk, the camera catches Jackson in the process of signing the register. By the time the cycle repeats, Jackson is moving into the elevator.

Kowalski asks, "Do you want me to stop it?"

"No. Keep going. I want to see if anyone comes in after him."

As the tape ran forward, Kowalski posed a question. "Maybe the killer was already in the hotel?"

I shake my head. "I don't think so. The guy's driving a rental car, stops for the night, and picks this hotel for a reason. He was gonna meet someone. On the flip side, I think someone followed him." I point toward the screen. "I'll bet we see the murderer right there."

Kowalski places his empty coffee cup to the side and takes control of the VCR. "I'm gonna fast forward it."

I mumble an incoherent acknowledgment and reached for my second serving.

The programmed sequence of the security continued its rounds. After several cycles, the front desk came back into view and Doug McGuire was not at his post. When it finally returns to the lobby view, we glimpse a woman, assisted by a crutch, getting into the elevator. Again, Doug was absent.

"If that's our suspect, we should see her leaving, too," says Kowalski.

"Yeah," I agree. "And I don't think we'll have to wait too long if the coroner's estimate is correct."

"Let it run, Jack. I gotta take a pee. If you see our suspect, freeze it. I'm going to get some more coffee. Do you want a cup?"

"Yeah, but wash your hands first."

When Kowalski returns, he is holding two Styrofoam cups of steaming coffee. "Here ya go, Jack. Oh, I forgot to wash my hands, but I'm sure it's okay to drink," he says with a devious smile.

"That's okay, Stan. I forgot to tell you, I sample-licked all the donuts. So, I guess we're even." I point at the frozen screen. "I see you found our person of interest. Looks like she's taking a powder out the side door."

"Yep. The timestamp is 11:48 p.m.," says Kowalski before handing the cup to me.

"I see she left using the side entrance. Look, she's got an accomplice," I remarked. The leading beams of light from an approaching car highlight her hair as she pushes her way outside. Before we could get a good look at the car, the camera switched views.

"Did you notice anything different?"

Kowalski nods. "Yeah, she didn't have her crutch."

"Which means she ditched it somewhere in the hotel. We gotta get back there before the evidence disappears."

Chapter Seven

Doug shuffles past the empty pool and through the remains of a mediocre snow removal job and climbs his way to the second story. Reaching his apartment, he stomps off snow that had collected on the tops of his shoes, then pushes past the putrid yellow door and into his apartment. No matter how many times he passed it, the thought of smothering it under a heavy coat of red paint crosses his mind. The only thing that stops him was the fear of being homeless in December—well, for that matter, any month.

Doug drops his car keys in a Route 66 souvenir dish that was left behind by a tourist who apparently checked out of the hotel with little concern for retaining it. Actually, much of Doug's possessions were hotel guests' castoffs or lost and found unclaimed treasures. He set his backpack off to the side before removing his parka and drapes it on one of the mismatched kitchen chairs. He pulls out the other chair, sits down, then unlaces his shoes before kicking them aside.

Now in stocking feet, he walks toward his only expensive piece of furniture, a credenza that he managed to retain in the divorce settlement. Not that he had to put up much of a fuss because his wife, Sheila hated it the day he brought it home. She said it was tacky, claiming, in her words, "It is ugly brown. And those stupid carvings don't match the rest of our stuff." Well, it didn't match the rest of his present furnishing either, which was a mixture of Danish modern, Mediterranean, and cheap. But it also served as an excellent spot for his Admiral black-and-white TV. With a flick of the switch, he heard the *Ballad of Gilligan's Isle* as the screen gradually came to life.

Doug goes back to his kitchen set, picks up his bag, and moves it to the side of his sleeper couch, where he plops himself down across its entire length. Sometimes, when he's in a funk, this will be his bedtime position—too lazy to open the sleeper. Right now, his mind is on other things. Sluggishly, he reaches into his rucksack, pulls out the mysterious envelope, and sets it on his chest. He tilts the envelope toward himself, and allows its contents to spill onto his shirt. He snatches up the key, capturing it before it slides off onto the carpeted floor. With great interest, he studies its shape.

Once, when a locksmith came to the hotel, Doug picked his brain about the various parts of locks and keys. It wasn't anything more than his curiosity as an amateur sleuth wanting material for one of his novels. He remembers the term "bow" of the key, where all the information is stamped. This key, thicker than most, was stamped with the manufacturer's name, Francis Keil & Sons. The reverse side had only the number 209 hand-stamped and decorative scrolling along its bow. Besides the markings, the most notable thing was its severe wear—meaning ... it had to be much older than Doug.

Drawn by the laughter from the television, Doug turns to his left and glimpses Ginger doing a makeover on a woman who came to the island to escape society.

Yeah, I know the feeling.

He sets the key off to the side of the couch and grabs the matchbook.

Two Guns? It's a ghost town—burned out nine years ago, now only a curiosity on the way to Winslow, or westbound to Flagstaff. I was a senior in high school when it happened. We all took a trip there to see what happened—only a few buildings now, and those pretty much trashed. The old matchbook ... it's from the motel that died in the big fire. Obviously, it's important enough to kill someone, and that's the rub.

An Excuse to Kill

The matchbook joins the key on the floor, and Doug pulls the comforter off the top of his couch, covers himself, and closes his eyes.

Chapter Eight

It was close to noon as Kowalski and I approached the registration counter of the Double Six Hotel. Phyllis, by the tag on her jacket's lapel, looks up from her paperwork and greets us with a smile. Returning the unspoken greeting, I flash my badge. Her smile wavers.

"Good morning, sir. I suppose you want to talk with my manager, Sharon MacFarlane?"

With a nod, I reply, "But before you call your manager, do you have a lost and found?"

She laughs. "What hotel doesn't? You'd be surprised how much stuff people leave behind. Hang on a sec, I'll page Sharon." She reaches for the telephone, punches in a few numbers, and relays our request.

Smiling, Phyllis returns the handset and asks, "Is there something in particular you are looking for?"

I answer, "Crutches."

She lets out a huff. "Yeah, Juanita, one of our housemaids, found a pair of crutches in the stairwell. Who leaves crutches behind? I mean, if you need them, you need them ... unless they got healed between the third and first floor. This place isn't like Fatima. You know what I mean?"

I nod, thankful she ran out of breath.

The elevator opens, and Sharan Macfarlane moves with purpose in our direction. She extends her hand. "Detectives, what can I do for you?"

Taking her hand in mine, I say, "We came here to see if any of your staff came across some unclaimed crutches."

Releasing her grasp, she shook her head. "Not to my knowledge, but perhaps—"

"No need to go on, Ms. Macfarlane. Your desk clerk informed us just now that they placed a pair in your lost and found."

I could see her turn a shade of pink. "Oh ... it's not something I would keep track of."

Kowalski chimes in. "Do you have a separate room for those things?"

Macfarlane laughs. "Although we get our share of items left behind, we only need one shelf. Thirty days, then whoever wants it gets it. We keep them in our utility room. Come this way."

We trail behind Macfarlane as she leads us down the first-floor hallway. Using her passkey, she unlocks the door, and we follow her in. I catch a whiff of bleach and Pine-Sol. The room is spacious with a large washer and dryer, a sorting table, shelving filled with bedding and towels. The ample remaining space tells me it was intended for additional gear.

I ask, "Do you do all your laundry with only those two machines?"

She laughs. "No, only occasionally. An outside contractor does most of our laundry. We only have sixty rooms. So, employing additional staff to do the laundry would only hurt our bottom line."

I continue to examine the room's layout. "Just out of curiosity, how many housekeepers do you employ?"

Macfarlane starts for the side wall, where I can see the crutches leaning against the gray shelving. "Our regular staff has fifteen, but during skiing season, like now, we have twenty."

She reaches for the crutches.

"Ms. Macfarlane, let me get that," says Kowalski, beating her to the shelf. He grabs them with one swoop of his massive latex glove-encased hand. "We don't want any more fingerprints on them than we have already."

Macfarlane backs away and nods. "Of course."

"And speaking about fingerprints, I'd like to have your housekeeper, Juanita, stop by the station for a fingerprinting."

"She's here now. You can tell her yourself, Detective. If we're done, I can go find her and bring her to the office, if that's okay with you?"

"Sure. Actually, I want to ask her if she was the only one to handle them."

Macfarlane starts for the exit.

"Before we go, you say that you employ around fifteen to twenty housekeeping staff. Are they regulars, or do you have a big turnover?"

"It's a mix, but we get several of our help from the Hopi Indians and a few Havasupai. Not all live on the reservations. Also, some come from the Hispanic community. It's kind of hard, though. We are competing with the other businesses who work in the tourist trade."

I ask, "What keeps them coming back to your operation?"

"I think it's the tips and steady income. Also, I try to be flexible with their needs. Not everybody does that around here. If that's all, Detective, we can go to my office, and I'll fetch Juanita."

We continue to her office, passing Phyllis, who was diligently making entries into the hotel's computer terminal.

Macfarlane waved us in, then departed.

Kowalski leans the crutches against the wall and sits down. "Owens, you think that maybe this was an inside job, like maybe one of the cleaning people had something to do with the hit?"

I take a seat from across the desk. "Nope. I'm thinking of all the angles. But, considering the hitman, in this case a woman, didn't appear to need any help. She just strolled in, did her job, and left."

The door opens, and I glance up, believing it was Macfarlane. Instead, it was Phyllis who pokes her head around the door.

"Ah, I don't know if this is important, but someone came into the hotel and asked about the man who died."

"You mean right now?" I ask, thinking we have a major break in the case.

"No, yesterday."

In my disbelief, I got up and stood facing her. "And you didn't think it was important to notify us until now?"

"I was kind of busy. He thanked me for telling him what happened, then left." She shrugs. "That's all."

I think she's a bimbo and lucky to have this job—no, any job. "What time was that?" I ask in my less-than-charitable tone.

She looks as if she's about to cry. "I relieved Doug, so ... that would have been shortly after eight."

Still, in my bad-cop frame of mind, I ask, "Did he say anything else?"

"No ... I mean ... he did ask who was on duty that night?"

"And, of course, you told him, right?"

Her lower lip quivers. "Yeah ... I didn't think—"

"That's right, you didn't think."

Yep, now the tears.

Chapter Nine

Doug McGuire's own snoring woke him. The apartment is cold. Wrapping the comforter around himself like an Indian woman, while avoiding stepping on the envelope and its contents, he swings off the couch. Shuffling his way toward the thermostat, he adjusts the temperature and gently taps it a few times. There's a metallic click.

His lifestyle on the graveyard shift has transformed him into a coffee addict. He moves to the sink, where he fills the glass carafe before pouring its contents into his drip coffee maker. Measuring out several scoops of coffee into the filter, he pushes a button that begins to glow bright red, then heads to the bathroom.

After a hot shower, he towels off and then dresses in jeans and a red and black checkered flannel shirt. Skipping his shave out of rebellion for the routine imposed on him by the demands of his job, he looks into his mirror, then rubs his stubble with satisfaction and smiles.

He sniffs the air and heads for the coffeemaker. Now holding a steaming cup in his hand, he goes to the credenza and, rummaging through one of its drawers, he locates an Arizona roadmap. Doug sleeps in on his one weekend a month off, but with a mysterious death and tempting clues, that's about to change. He diligently spreads the map on his kitchen table, smoothing out the worn folds. Using an index finger, he follows I-40 until he reaches Two Guns.

Let's see, that's only about a forty-mile drive. Easy peasy.

He moves toward the kitchen cabinets, reaches up, and opens one of the doors. Tiptoed and, with some effort, he pulls down a shoebox from the top shelf and places it on the counter. Removing the lid, he pulls out a Harrington & Richardson .22 caliber revolver, thinking; *I don't know what I'm getting into, but this might come in handy.* Using the ejector rod, he frees the cylinder from the frame and sets the revolver aside.

Once more, he reaches into the box and lifts out a nearly full container of .22 caliber long rifle ammo. Doug grabs a handful, picks up the gun, and begins to chamber nine rounds. His apartment still has a chill, yet his hands perspire. Once loaded, he attempts to secure the cylinder with a quick twist of his wrist, the way he saw movie cowboys do. It doesn't work, and a couple of bullets fall onto the counter. Returning the rounds, he secures the cylinder but without the theatrics.

The last time he used the gun was several months ago. He and his high school buddy Ralph went out to the low country to target-shoot or sometimes kill an occasional rattlesnake. Because of his work hours, Doug and Ralph can only get together once a month, that is, if it fits with Ralph's schedule. Doug's wife, Sheila, hated Ralph and did everything in her power to discourage their relationship. Now, it wasn't a problem.

Doug considered telling his buddy about the envelope, but decided it was too early in the venture to risk revealing his secret. Thinking about the envelope, with a cup of coffee in hand, he heads toward the couch. He sets his cup on the side table, then stoops down to pick up the envelope along with its diverse paraphernalia. He squeezes the envelope between his thumb and index finger, blows a hearty breath into the gap to widen its slender opening, and notices something previously overlooked.

Maybe I need Ralph after all?

Chapter Ten

Emily Ruger looks up from her desk as Kowalski and I entered the cramped evidence room. Her usual smile was absent. Since her transfer from Phoenix a few months ago, her overall assimilation into our branch has been positive. So, her gray mood wasn't like her. Although I couldn't figure out why she made the move in the first place, considering it was more of a step down than a career boost. Now, as far as I was concerned, she brightened my day with her Sally Field charm alongside a modicum of sassiness accented by her auburn shag hairstyle.

"We brought you another present from the Double Six Hotel case," I say with a tinge of sarcasm while Kowalski, holding the crutches, trails behind.

"Thanks a lot, you two. I'll add it to my growing collection of evidence."

"You finding anything interesting?" I ask, surprised by her announcement of the increase.

"You betcha. Besides the two slugs, we found a couple of strands of hair that we suspect came from the shooter and a decent boot print under the toilet tank."

"Under the toilet tank?" asks Kowalski while propping our additional evidence against Ruger's desk.

"Yeah. Grayson Donelly figured it came from the woman straddling the toilet bowl as she lifted the tank cover. Yep, she was careless by failing to wipe her boots when she came in from the outside."

I ask, "You're sure she made those imprints?"

"Hey, that's our business and our call. The prints matched nothing the victim had. We figure she comes in, does her business, and then starts searching. She goes past the body and into the bathroom first because it's the most overlooked hiding place. But, considering the hit, she's a pro and does things differently than most."

I joke, "Not pro enough to leave boot prints, though."

"Yeah. We figured it was the initial spot. If she had looked in the bed area first, which was carpeted, her wet boots might have dried by then. And considering the amount of snow we had, she was probably carrying snow up to the top of her boots. If I were looking for a hiding spot, I would go for the back of the toilet tank or taped to the inside lid."

"I'd say you got lucky."

Ruger laughed. "Luck has nothing to do with it. It's more of us outwitting the criminal mind. You know those hotel rugs aren't exactly done by Mr. Clean—there's a lot of dirt trapped in those fibers. So, what's with the crutches?"

Kowalski, standing off to the side and leaning on a file cabinet, says, "We figured the killer used it as a prop to gain sympathy and access to Jackson's room. She left them in the stairwell."

"Yeah," I add. "The old damsel-in-distress ploy."

"Probably not going to find anything if she left it behind," says Ruger, getting up from her chair. "My guess is they'll have the prints of whoever found them—that's it."

"Maybe," I answer, "but we have a grainy photograph of her, which may be enough. We'll hit the hockshops and see if anyone can recall selling them."

Ruger scoffs. "Lots of luck. You know, crutches and skis are almost ubiquitous around these parts."

"Even with the less-than-perfect photo, she's got a build, and I'm counting on someone remembering her."

"You guys are all alike," mocks Ruger. "My guess is if she's that good-looking, whoever sold her the crutches didn't look any higher than her chin."

"Well, that may be true of other guys, but I admire women for their brains."

I hear Kowalski choke.

Ruger snickers. "Hey, before it gets too deep and I have to shovel my way out of here, I gotta get back to work."

"Sure, we'll get out of your hair, but before we do, how about a picture of the crutches?"

"Okay, if you want a couple of eight-by-ten glossies, it will take me more time than I got to give. But if you want the down and dirty, I'll get out my Polaroid SX-70."

"Give me the down and dirty," I say with a smirk, which, by her body language, she doesn't appreciate. *I'm not going to win her favor if I don't lose the Bronx-cop-attitude.*

She slips on some latex gloves, grabs the evidence, and hurries off.

I sit on one of the two folding chairs while Kowalski continues to prop himself against the filing cabinet. "You know, Jack, if you want to get into her pants, you better ditch the smart-ass attitude."

"Who says I'm trying to get into her undies? Maybe she's trying to get into my skivvies by playing hard to get?"

Kowalski laughs and shakes his head. "I tell you, Jack, you got one hell of an ego. But in a perverted way, maybe that might appeal to the wrong sort of woman. My guess, being a happily married man, she is not that kind of woman."

I say, "Maybe you're right, considering I'm done with one already." I pick up one of the well-worn *True Police Cases* magazines, which, judging by Ruger's reaction, isn't her reading material.

We sat for several minutes while I marveled at the sight of bust sizes, and Kowalski quietly hummed a tune I had never heard, thinking it may have been from his church.

Ruger returned minus the crutches but waves three Polaroid photographs in her hand.

"Here ya go, gents. I did three shots: one for the entire set, one closeup of the manufacturer logo, and, ta, ta, the shop's sticker from under one of the armpit's supports. It's intended to be inconspicuous to prevent a fraudulent return."

I say, "Does it have a name imprint?"

"Yes, sir. The place is The Barn Guys, and from my limited knowledge of Flagstaff, its on the outskirts of town."

She hands me the prints. "Be careful. They still may be a little damp. Now that I've done your detective work, I need to get back to mine."

Her Sally Field charm returns.

Chapter Eleven

Doug McGuire dials his buddy Ralph. He answers on the third ring. "Ralph?"

"Yeah, my main man. Wassup?"

"I really need your help. You doing anything today?"

"Yeah, buddy, talking to you," Ralph says with a snicker in his voice.

"I mean, all day today?"

"Since you got rid of the Wicked Witch of the West, it's your call, buddy."

"Ralph, I've gotten myself into a mess, and I really need your help."

"Whadda do, man, waste someone?"

"No, but someone was killed."

"Whoa! I'm in, Buddy. Do you want me to come to your pad?"

"No. I think it's best if I come to your place."

"Bitchin'," says Ralph, and the line goes dead.

Expecting temperatures to be on the cool side in the desert, Doug pours the rest of the coffee from his carafe into his thermos. He then screws down the cup, remembering the not-so-secure seal, and giving it one last twist. Throwing the envelope, highway map, and gun into his rucksack, he puts on his jacket and Tucson Padres' baseball cap, one of his many hotel findings, and heads for the door. With the thermos in one hand, he drops the backpack onto the floor and opens the door, letting in a blast of cold air. Once outside, he tosses the pack, using only one strap, onto his right shoulder and locks up.

Doug's first car was a Volkswagen, which he later traded in for a yellow 1975 AMC Pacer. He thought it the coolest car ever and a sure chick magnet. *Motor Trend* magazine's hype as "the most innovative of all US small cars" convinced him of its value. Later, tagged as the '70 ugly car, it was mocked in the movie *Wayne's World,* further sealing its fate as never being a pickup car. Well, he did score with his wife, a result of its roomy interior, but that was another story.

With the bag slung on his right shoulder and cradling his thermos in the same hand, Doug takes one step at a time to the ground level, mindful of the slick covering of snow. Shuffling his way to his car, parked in front of his apartment, he approached it from the passenger side. He opens the door and inconspicuously removes the revolver from his bag and slips it into the glove compartment. Laying the backpack on the floor, he wedges the thermos between it and the center console.

Once on the driver's side, he starts the Pacer's engine, mentally encouraging the gas needle to flee from the red zone. Although considered a compact car, it wasn't easy on the gallon-to-mile ratio. Luckily, he still had Sam Jackson's fifty constrained in his wallet against his fiver and four singles of folding money.

The moment Doug started the car, he shot a stream of defrosting solution onto his window. After several swipes of the blades, he had a clear view. Before putting the Pacer into gear, he reaches for the radio but stopped short, preferring the silence. For the next fifteen minutes, he knew he had to tell Ralph everything, but he wasn't sure Ralph could keep it a secret.

As the windshield wipers pushes the backwash of other cars, he tried to keep pace with calculated applications of mixture with slush for fear of draining the reservoir of solution. It wasn't a matter of finding a place to fill it—it was more of not wanting to stop. He breathes a sigh of relief as he pulls off Highway 89 and into the campgrounds. Doug, now relaxed, follows the road, hearing only the crunch of tires on gravel until he pulls alongside Ralph's small trailer. Before getting out, he grabs his backpack but leaves behind the thermos and gun.

Doug locks the car and, out of caution, looks around, but doesn't notice the car that followed him from his apartment. Slinging his bag over his shoulder, he approaches Ralph's trailer door and knocks.

Chapter Twelve

The Barn Guys' place welcomes us with a whiff of vestige memories as Kowalski and I push our way in. The door chime alerts the proprietor of our presence. A quick glance at the place indicates it's a slow Saturday. The sales counter sits near the door, no doubt, for security reasons.

A middle-aged man gave us a perfunctory nod and went back to reading the *Arizona Daily Sun.*

As we approach, he puts down the paper with some reluctance, but his eyes pop a bit when we flash our shields.

"What can I do for you today, gentlemen?" he asks.

I remove the three Polaroids and place them on the glass counter. "I'm Detective Owens, and this is Detective Kowalski. We are looking for the buyer of these crutches. Their markings show they were purchased here."

The guy gives us a quick chuckle. "I'd like to help you, but can you give me some idea when? Also, I'm not the only one working the place. I have a partner, and we have a few part-time people, too."

Kowalski chimed in. "We're investigating a murder that occurred at the Double Six Hotel."

The man taps his newspaper. "Yeah, I was just reading about it. Really bad shit, and never good for the tourist trade."

Like a man laying down a couple of cards on a five-card draw, Kowalski drops the two grainy images of the woman suspect.

"Hey, man, I remember that babe. Who wouldn't with that figure?"

I say, "Do you recall the day?"

He hesitates. "Maybe five or six days ago. But if you have the time, you are welcome to have a look-see at my security tapes?"

Now, I don't think I lead a charmed life, but once in a while, I get lucky. "We have the time."

"Ah, my partner is out back in our workshop. I'll have to get him to man the counter. By the way, my name is Chet."

"Okay ... Chet, we'll wait," I say, happy to have a break in the case.

While Chet runs off, Kowalski says, "I think I'll look around to see if I can't find my wife something for Christmas."

"You mean you haven't gotten her anything yet? Christmas is only ten days away."

"Yah know this job doesn't always give me the opportunity to shop, Jack."

"Well, you look and shop, and I'll just look."

I have always enjoyed browsing these old places, looking at memories, like in a museum. The only difference is you can buy this stuff. So, I moseyed through the aisles while Kowalski shopped.

Chet comes back with his partner, Rick. We shook hands. Rick was now in charge, and Chet led us to the back room.

Like most storage and workshops, the place bulged with stuff. I saw only two folding chairs, which meant one of us would stand or share a chair. *I don't think so.*

Kowalski, the gentleman that he is, eased back and motioned to me to have the chair.

Pleased, I sat down because that's the kind of guy I am.

Chet points to the RCA monitor. "We switch videocassettes every six hours if we can remember. Then we pencil in the date. Sometimes, we don't really need to record because the cameras are enough to deter shoplifters. It's grainy black and white footage, but you can make out most of the details fairly well."

Kowalski says, "Chet, did you, by chance, remember the color of the woman's hair?"

"Oh, yeah. It was red, my favorite color."

"Mine, too."

We all laugh, and I say, "But, Stan, your wife Mary's a blonde?"

"Yeah, keep it under your hat."

My smile assures him I would.

Chet hits the play button. "I guess I'll have the recording somewhere in these four cassettes. With a jerking motion, figures fly across the screen, alternating views, while each camera takes a turn.

After an hour, my eyes hurt, and I rub them to get back in circulation.

Kowalski yells, "Stop!"

Bleary-eyed, I look up, and sure enough, even concealed in black and white footage, the red-headed bombshell strolls through the front door. It is a better view of her face, unlike the profile from the hotel's camera. She's wearing the same fur-lined coat but more cinched up.

She disappears, and we see her pop up here and there as she moves through the store. Although we didn't actually see her select the crutches, she appeared briefly at the front counter holding them.

I thought she'd be gone before the next cycle, but to my surprise, she lingered while Chet put the shmooze on her. We catch her paying. I noticed she was wearing gloves when she first came into the place. Now, as she dishes out cash, I notice a chunky lightning bolt ring wrapped around her right thumb. *We got you, sister!*

Chapter Thirteen

R alph's boisterous greeting spilled beyond his trailer. He waves a wide arc with his arm. "Hey, man, c'mon in."

It's barely above thirty degrees, and Ralph is wearing a gaudy Hawaiian shirt with beer in hand. Ever since Magnum, P.I, he adopted the Tom Selleck persona. Yep, my buddy is crazy, but he's my pal with lingo locked between Disco and the awesome era.

Doug drops his backpack alongside the doorway. It makes a hollow sound on the thin trailer's floor.

"Care for a brewski?" Ralph waves the can in the air.

Doug smiles. "It's a bit early for that. I think I've got to keep a clear head."

"You in trouble with the man?"

"Maybe."

"Legit?"

"I think so," says Doug as he slides into one of the stationary kitchen benches.

"Whoa! Lay it on me, man."

"Okay, but you cannot tell a soul. Got that?"

Ralph crosses his heart in a less-than-dignified manner. "Scout's honor."

Doug laughed. "You were never a scout."

"Bite me."

Doug leans forward on the table while Ralph slips into the opposite bench. "Okay, here's the story. This … ah, Sam Jackson, he checked into our hotel last week, and some guy pops him dead."

"Whoa! You shitting me?"

"No. Let me finish."

Ralph holds up his arms in submission.

"Okay, this guy gives me a fifty to keep an envelope in the hotel safe. I figure, what the hell. Well, the guy doesn't claim it because he's dead, which I didn't know when I left work. When I came back for my check, I found out what happened, and I got the third degree for using the safe."

"So, did you keep the envelope?"

"Yeah, I'll show you."

Doug reaches around the back of the bench and picks up his back-pack. With the bag on his lap, he unzips it and pulls out the envelope. He slides the contents onto the table, then pushes it toward Ralph.

"Okay, you got a matchbook from the old KOA camp with a bunch of numbers and a key stamped with the number 209. Wazzit all mean, man?"

"Dunno, but a man died for it. But I'm going to tell you something that'll blow your socks off."

"Dude, I'm all ears."

Doug pulls out a pocket knife, crouches down at eye level with the table, and carefully peels back the seal around the envelope. "I didn't notice the first time, but when I put everything back, I blew it open and noticed this." He undoes it and theatrically flattens open the inside of the envelope to expose a drawing.

"Whoa!"

"Yeah, whoa is right." Doug agrees.

Ralph waves the open envelope in the air. "Close the shades, man. You got a treasure map."

Chapter Fourteen

Kowalski and I step out of the Barn Guys' place and into the cold Flagstaff air.

"Now what, Jack?"

I wish I knew. Not wanting Stan to think I didn't have a plan, I reply in my usual self-assured way, "I'm still thinking."

"You mean you don't know, right?"

Wanting to show off my powers of analysis by not jumping to conclusions, I hum, biding some time, and perused the area. After doing a one-eighty, I looked back at the shop and caught sight of the camera over the entrance.

"Wait a minute, wait a minute. Remember when we were looking at the tape, and we saw the row of cars in front of the shop?"

"Yeah?"

"C'mon, as long as we are still here, let's go back and look at this tape again."

"Why?" says Kowalski.

"Because that gal's car may be on it, *and* we may be lucky enough to get a license plate number or make of car."

Kowalski gives me a nod.

As we turn, I say, "By the way, did you find your wife a Christmas present?"

Kowalski holds the door open. "I did, but in the excitement, I forgot to buy it. Thanks for reminding me."

Chet was once more at his counter. He looked up in surprise. "Forget something?"

I say, "In a way. I'd like to use your recorder and have another look-see."

Chet flips a thumb backward. "Rick's in the back. You know the way."

I linger near the counter while Kowalski does the deal.

Kowalski hesitates near the front case and points. "Ah, before we leave, I'd like to purchase that pearl brooch."

A smile forms on Chet's face. "You got it. Do you want me to gift wrap it? It's not a big deal. We do that for our customers this time of year. Do you want to know the price?"

"Nah. My wife really likes that kind of stuff."

Already on my way back, Kowalski catches up with me.

I say, "You're one hell of a husband."

"I have one hell of a wife."

I knock on the workshop door then push my way in.

We interrupt Rick, who was leaning over his workbench, involved in what looked like a repair job. "Back so soon?"

I say, "I have another favor to ask you."

"You got the floor."

"I know we have the tape, but to save some time, I'd like to go over it again around the time of the sale."

"Sure. What are you expecting to find?"

"I want to look at the outside footage—particularly the parked cars."

Rick says, "Gimme the tape."

After installing it, Rick locates the spot and advances the footage.

I say, "Only pause at the outside cars."

"Look, Jack. Right there, on the right, it's a black Pontiac Turbo Trans AM," says Kowalski.

I nod. "Yep, even on a black-and-white screen, black pops black."

Kowalski says, "That bumper on the Trans sticks out a bit and partially blocks the plate."

I say, "It's a California plate."

Rick says, "I don't know, but the first letter is R, and the second one a B or E?"

I nod. "I agree. You got good eyes, Rick."

Kowalski points at the monitor. "Do you realize how many plates begin with an R and have a B or E attached?"

"I know, but we have a major clue. Considering the crime, I think our perp is still going to hang around until she gets what she wants. My bet is she doesn't know we know. We'll put out an APB and see what comes of it."

Chapter Fifteen

Ralph rose, threw his empty beer can into the open mouth of his trash container, which already exceeded capacity, and almost tittered out. He takes out a replenishment from his refrigerator. "Doug, still hanging dry?"

"Yeah," he says, looking back at the crude hand-drawn map.

Ralph slips back onto his kitchen table's bench and takes hold of the sta-tab on his beer and pulls. Foam spills over the edge of the can.

Doug looks up and says, "Listen, Ralph, before you pull that, I want you to come with me today to check this out."

"So?"

"I need you sober. How many of those did you have this morning?"

"Take a chill pill. Two."

"How many?"

"Okay, okay, maybe three." He takes his hand away from the can.

"The sun's gonna set around a quarter after five today. So, if we get going, we should have enough time to at least look at the area."

"What about eating?" says Ralph.

"We can stop at Mr. Bob's and get a quick bite."

"Deal," says Ralph.

"One more thing. By any chance, you got a compass?"

"Like when I was a Boy Scout?"

Doug laughs. "Yeah, like when you were a scout."

"I scarfed one out of the trash while on my trash route some time back."

"Good. Go get it. Where're gonna need it."

"Groovy!"

* * *

Doug eases his Pacer car off Interstate 40 at exit 230. He slowly makes his way toward an abandoned gas station, which is coated with layers of graffiti. In front of the station and under its canopy, a vintage model Chevy sits in its shade. No one seems to be in the car, but Doug figures by its condition, it's not junker.

Ralph points toward the distant skeletal remains of the old KOA Kamp. "Hey, man. You know, that old matchbook cover of yours is a clue."

"Yeah, I know. We'll head out over there."

Passing the station on their left, they guide right and park near a long-ago, water-filled cement pool. Like the gas station, the pool is clustered with bright graffiti. Doug is the first to get out. Both of them stretch and survey the area.

"Well, buddy, what do you think?" asks Doug.

"Damn, it's cold. I should have worn my flannel shirt," he says, zipping up his Parker coat.

"I mean, about the situation?"

"Far out, man ... far out."

Doug walks to the main structure while Ralph follows.

Pausing before the bony edifice, Doug says, "This must be the starting point. It has to make sense."

"Man, I'm stoked." Ralph blurts out, "We could be millionaires."

Doug shakes his head. "That may be a bit too ambitious of an amount."

"Let's think about it. This must be the starting point. Maybe in the middle?"

"Nah, man. It's got to be ... right in the center of that. See, the X on the map is away from this building ... it's there." Ralph points to the pool's steps."

Doug hurries to the pool and eases his way toward its center.

"Here, man, take the compass."

Doug isn't expecting Ralph to throw it, and Doug almost drops it. "You could have warned me?"

"Yeah, yeah. Don't freak out. Now, there is this number: 327.31° and 659.61 yards. It sounds like maybe it's an angle like on that compass. Open it up and see what 327° points to."

"No, 327.31°, but my compass can't split hairs," says Doug as he flips up two sides of the compass and lines them up with the magnetic north. He eyeballs 327°. He points in a general direction. "It's over there."

"You're pointing toward that frontage road, but I can't say if it's close to being 659 yards," says Ralph.

"That's gotta be the first clue," Doug says, looking into the distance. "We got more numbers to check out.".

"C'mon, Ralph, let's check out that road."

The two treasure seekers return to the Pacer and head toward the Interstate, but turn and move along the frontage road. Passing the abandoned gas station on the right, Doug notices the vintage Chevy is gone. It's been replaced by a black Trans AM. He thinks nothing of the man and woman who are inside. His wheels grind away at the loose gravel while the sun races west.

Chapter Sixteen

Kowalski and I go back to the station. It's probably too early, but we check with the board and dispatcher if any leads have come in. Nothing.

I remark, "It's been a long day, and I'm beat. I'm gonna call it a night. I've got a big day tomorrow."

"Like what?" asks Kowalski.

"Like, it's Sunday, and I have to do my laundry."

"Jack, if you want, you could come over to our place for supper and a few beers."

"Sounds inviting, but I need to keep up with my domestic chores."

"Suit yourself, but Mary is expecting you to come over sometime during the holidays."

"I will. I promise." *I know I say that, but I find it a bit depressing with Kowalski's family life and mine, well, like being in the shitter.*

Kowalski waves off and leaves.

My first inclination was to stop for a scotch, but I decided against it, opting instead to stay with my stock, which included propping myself up on the couch.

The front desk had the usual: a drunk sandwiched between two uniformed officers, a young couple being interviewed off to the side, and a guy with a clipboard in hand filling out a report. In passing, I wave at the duty clerk, but he's too focused to respond.

Tired, I push myself outside and tighten the belt on my overcoat against the sharpness of the night air. There's a dusting of snow on my windshield. My wipers dispatch it with a few swipes, aided by a shot of cleaner, which forms a thin layer of ice over the glass before succumbing to the car's defroster.

As I travel north, I see the frivolity of Flagstaff's nightlife, its orange, warming glow spilling onto the snow-dusted streets, and everyone boisterously enjoying themselves. The party atmosphere soon fades as my car slips into the residential area.

My condo is on the second floor. I picked that because, first—I don't like anyone running over my ceiling, and second—I liked the view. The place has one bedroom, which is enough considering my social status. It has a washer and dryer, helping maintain my self-imposed quarantine from noisy laundromats and troublesome rolls of quarters.

Coming in from the front balcony, I flip my overcoat onto an easy chair near the fireplace, which I start, and kick off my loafers. The accouterments of my single life include a few cacti, my choice because they don't need a lot of watering, pictures of the surrounding mountains, and a stereo for mood music. I also have a rather enormous trunk that sits in front of the couch. I liked the looks of it. It also serves as storage for things I have no idea where to put them.

I remove my sports coat and hang it on one of the kitchen chairs. Focused on that drink I promised myself, I open the liquor cabinet, pour a scotch, and chill it with an ice cube. Swirling the cube, it tinkles. I take a satisfying sip.

As I ease myself onto the couch, I hear a trail of footsteps approach the top landing. Still carrying the Smith & Wesson .38 Special in my shoulder holster, I swing out and go to the door. *Maybe it's Kowalski insisting I come for dinner. Nah, he'd call.*

Now, life is full of surprises, and being a cop arms you with a sixth sense. So, I open the door, and beside the blast of cold air, I run smack dab into the unexpected—my ex-wife, which sends more of a chill down my spine than the Flagstaff air.

"Hey, Jack," she says, looking every bit the ogre I remember leaving in New York, only a bit thinner.

"Jessica?"

"You still remember my name, Jack. It's cold out here. You gonna invite me in?"

I pull the door and allow her to pass. She rubbernecks the place and does an approving hum. "Not bad, not bad. You did pretty good for yourself."

"I manage. I just poured myself a scotch. Do you want one?"

"Of course. You shouldn't drink alone."

"And speaking of being alone, are you here in Flagstaff by yourself?"

"Babs and I came here for the holidays to see for ourselves what this town is all about. You remember Babs?"

"How could I ever forget? Is she still working for the DA's office?"

"Yeah."

I walk to the liquor cabinet, thinking about how I hated Babs, the know-it-all bigmouth who negatively influenced Jessica. I grab a glass, pour the drink, and then offer it to her.

"Enough?"

She nods.

"Ice?"

She nods again.

I go to the freezer. "And where is Babs now?"

"She met this cute guy at one of the ski lodges."

"And you? Seeing anyone?"

"I keep my options open."

I drop in two cubs and hand her the drink. She moves to the couch. After kicking off her heels, she draws up her legs and leans against the inside arm.

I ask, "How long are you gonna be in Flagstaff?"

"Till after Christmas."

There's a long pause, and I'm wishing my couch would swallow her.

"Say, Jack, I thought we could get together and have dinner, you know, talk about old times?"

"Jessica, I'm up to my eyeballs in a murder case, and frankly, right after I have my drink, I'm going to call it a night."

She takes a long drink and smacks her lips, an annoying habit I always disliked.

"I know this is a surprise for you, but can't we put bygones behind us?"

"It's nothing personal. I'm tired. Unless you have something to tell me ... ."

Her mouth drops slightly. "Ah, I've been diagnosed with breast cancer, and I wanted to clear the air between us."

Chapter Seventeen

The AMC Pacer eases its way past the Apache Death Camp.

"Ya know, that cave has always been kinda spooky," says Ralph, looking past Doug and out toward the location on their left.

Doug nods. "I know. They say the place is haunted."

"Well, they say the ghosts of dead Apache prowl here at night—real freaky-deaky stuff. Keep on steppin' man."

"Don't worry, Ralph, we're on a mission."

Their car continues, occasionally avoiding chunks of rock and trash.

"I think this is the place," says Doug. "Let's get out and check the road."

Ralph and Doug make their way to the center.

"Okay," Doug begins, "The angle has to have some starting point. I would guess it would be from the center."

Ralph points. "The matchbook says, 'Lion?'"

"Yeah, so what?"

"I'm stoked. Don't you get it, man? You got that bodacious hole in the center of that old ruin that says 'Mountain Lions.' Get my drift?"

"Yep, I do. Okay, let's get back in the car and go over there," says Doug.

Once at the ruins, both men eagerly jump out of the car and head for the weathered doorway. Doug says, "Take out your compass and use that angle from the envelope to see where it points."

Ralph, standing in the archway, shoots an imaginary line. "Dunno. I can't really see all that well. The matchbook says, 'water tower.' So, I'm guessing that old tank has got to be the spot. And the angle is kinda close to what the matchbook says."

"Okay, but does it mean the treasure is there?" says Doug.

"All we did was get a bunch of angles. Now what?" asks Ralph.

"Listen, we've come so far already. The sun's gonna set in a couple of hours. Let's eyeball the area."

"Fine by me. I'm freezin' my ass off. I'm ready to get back into the car." Without waiting for Doug, he heads for the car.

Doug, now crouching behind the wheel of the Pacer, continues to dodge road debris as he guides his way down the road. "Ralph, I don't think that small compass of yours is really going to be accurate enough for us to get any true bearings."

"What you getting at, man?"

"Whoever made those notes had something better than a Cub Scout compass. And they probably didn't use magnetic north but geographic north. Those figures are more precise than you can record from a simple compass. I figure a surveying crew made it, or at least someone who had the skills."

"Bummer. So, you think we have to hire someone?"

"They do have to have some sort of degree. I don't suppose you know of anyone?"

"There's this guy on my route," says Ralph. "He's an alright kinda dork, though."

"How do you read him? Can he be trusted?"

"I'm not sure, man. I see him once in a while. We shoot the shit, and that's it. He's a bit kooky, doesn't say too much, but is smart," says Ralph.

"We can't afford to pay him. We'd have to let him in on the deal."

"I almost think we'd have to, man."

Making their way, they move in the general direction toward what Doug considered to be the water tank, their intended target. Rather than take the shortest distance over the rough terrain, Doug backtracks and stays on the partially finished road.

Continuing along the pitted way, Doug says, "I'm a bit uneasy about this. We're going back the same way we started."

"This road takes us past the abandoned gas station," says Ralph.

Doug says, "I'm just worried about getting a flat tire in this stuff."

Having reached the tank, Doug shuts off the engine and opens the door.

Ralph slips out of the passenger side and zips up his coat.

Neither man hesitates. They head for the water tank and start circling it, kicking up dirt with the subconscious thought of uncovering the treasure.

Doug points. "Ralph, somewhere around here, is our fortune."

"Man, this is a pretty big area to start digging for treasure. Something about this doesn't make sense."

Doug says, "We're only looking at the general area. We can get in touch with your pal and narrow it down."

"Ten-four, good buddy."

Chapter Eighteen

I was debating whether I should tell Kowalski about my night visitor. Actually, I was having a difficult time accepting the news. I thought I'd put it on the back burner for now.

We had set up our crime board right after the death of Sam Jackson, who was undoubtedly an alias. The guy's morgue picture didn't flatter him, and, of course, they never do. With Jackson in the center, we began a web of joining clues. The woman with the thick lightning bolt ring got the highest billing, followed by the guy who inquired about Jackson. With the help of Phyllis Logan's description, our forensic artist put together a promising lead. As far as a possible capture on the security system, unbeknownst to us, and by accident, the hotel shut off the cameras after giving us the tape. Now, the trouble was, did he stay around, knowing of Jackson's death?

Kowalski looked at me the way he usually does right before asking me some personal questions. "You've been pretty quiet. Something bothering you?"

I knew he wasn't about to let up. If I told him about Jessica, it would be a distraction from our case.

"There is something, but let's wait until lunch."

"Well, now you got my interest. I hope you're not leaving and taking a job in Nome, Alaska?"

"Flagstaff is cold enough for me. I was thinking more like a job in the tropics." Hopefully, that will keep him at bay. I added the crutches to the board and connected the string. I included the Pontiac Turbo Trans AM.

"Jack, we're under the assumption the killer didn't find what they were looking for."

"That room was torn apart, with every nook and cranny searched. Although it is possible that she found what she was looking for, the law of averages suggests otherwise."

"I know what you mean," says Kowalski. "She trashes the entire hotel room, and at the very last place our killer looks, she locates the object of the hunt."

I tapped the drawing of the man who questioned Phyllis Logan. "This guy could help break this case. Every one of our patrols has a copy. Maybe we'll get lucky."

As Kowalski and I explore our options, Emily Ruger walks into our office. "Gentlemen, I believe I have something that may interest you."

I watch her saunter over to Kowalski's desk as she plunks down something. I admire the way she saunters. She points to the desk. "I found that tucked away in one of Jackson's pockets. Next time you two detectives go on a donut run, make sure you include one for me, even though I'm not a donut fan."

With the grace of a gazelle, she exists without another word.

I'm definitely in love.

Obviously, her theatrical display piques our interest, and we converge on Kowalski's desk.

I arrive first and pick up an old matchbook cover from a KOA camp in Two Guns, Arizona. I flip it open and see the number 230 scribbled on the inside flap. I hand it to Kowalski. "What do you make of this?"

"Yeah, the place is a ghost town now. Back in 1971, the year I joined the force in Flagstaff, that's why I remember it, the gas station in Two Guns burned down."

"When I go to Winslow or Holbrook, I'm always tempted to stop and check the place out."

Kowalski laughs. "Not much there now except rundown buildings covered in graffiti. Of course, though, there is the Apache death cave."

The name alone prompts me to ask, "Apache death cave?"

"Yep, there was a group of Apache raiders who attacked a Navajo encampment back around ... I think 1878. Anyway, it was almost a total slaughter of every man, woman, and child—except three young girls."

I ask, "Did this happen in Two Guns?"

"No, somewhere else, but it ended there. See, the raiding party took refuge there. The Navajo were pissed and gathered their own raiding party. They located the Apache in a cave at Two Guns and basically suffocated them by setting fire to the entrance while shooting blindly into the opening of the cave."

"You're a regular historian."

"When we first arrived here after leaving Milwaukee, we hit all the tourist spots, the Barringer Meteor Crater, Sedona's gift shops, and the Petrified Forest. Now my kids want to go to Phoenix or LA."

I ask, "Getting back to this matchbook, what do you make of it?"

With a conniving smile, he says, "Yah know, Jack, I just realized what this might be all about."

"Out with it. Don't keep me in suspense."

"Treasure—buried treasure."

"What, like *Treasure Island*, treasure?"

"Sort of. One story I remember in particular was back in 1889, when a group of settlers robbed a stagecoach east of Tucson. The haul was over $28,000. When they captured them, they only had $100—"

"Hold on a second," I say. "Interested as I am about hidden treasure, you're telling me, just by that matchbook cover, this whole business involves some sort of treasure involving a stagecoach going back to 1889?"

"That's only one account. Between 1875 and 1903, there were over 125 stagecoach robberies in Arizona."

"I'm glad I wasn't a detective back then."

"Jack, searching for that money is popular among treasure hunters around here. It's like hunting for Confederate gold or Blackbeard's treasure. It's all about the hunt and the prospect of getting rich. The matchbook is only a clue that buried treasure is involved."

I say, "Okay, say you're right. Now that you think you have the reason for Jackson's death, what now?"

"We need to find Jackson's relationship to this."

"Stan, what do you suggest?"

"We go through the library's archives. Maybe we'll find a connection."

Chapter Nineteen

It was a typical Sunday for El Paso Drive, with nothing stirring except for a few dogs yapping, probably wanting to escape the cold. Doug McGuire and Ralph Tyler stood outside the home of Cody Dosela. The small front yard had a collection of three vehicles, two of which were definitely not in working order, and the third was a road-salt and dirt-encrusted red and white 1979 Ford Bronco. The single-story house was trim-looking without embellishments other than a large dreamcatcher, which hung prominently on the right side of the door.

Ralph Tyler opens the screen door and then knocks. From inside, shuffling feet advance before the door flies open. Cody Dosela, an imposing, over six-foot native American, stands before him in stocking feet, dressed in jeans and a long-sleeved wool shirt with a white, gray, and light blue plaid pattern.

Cody eyes Ralph and then shoots a distrustful stare at Doug. "What you want?"

Ralph clears his throat and then gestures behind him. "Hey man, this is Doug. We got a business deal for you that will blow your mind."

Again, Cody glances at Doug and then says, "C'mon in."

After inviting Ralph and Doug in, Cody holds his ground. The pair squeeze past him and then stand off to the side.

Cody turns toward them and says, "Take off your shoes and come inside."

The house's warm interior is gloomy because of the drawn shades and blinds, plus the dark paneling adds to the drabness. Jutting out of the walls is a collection of indigenous wildlife, presumably the work of Cody.

Now shoeless, both men stand awkwardly, waiting for the next command.

Without an utterance, Cody motioned toward the couch.

The pair quickly follow the unsaid command.

Cody sits opposite them and says, "What business deal do you talk about?

Ralph nudges Doug.

Doug clears his throat, strikes the left side of his chest, and says, "We think we have a treasure map."

"Let me see," demands Cody, holding out his hand.

Doug hesitantly pulls out the map and hands it to him.

After a long pause and intense scrutiny, Cody finally says, "Why did you show me this? Where's the treasure?"

Doug takes the matchbook out of his shirt pocket and hands it to Cody.

Cody eyes the numbers and nods.

Ralph chimes in, "We need a surveyor. This could be a mega treasure, man."

"We can split it three ways," says Doug.

Cody returns the map and matchbook to Doug and says, "Forty percent for me."

Doug and Ralph exchange glances.

"Whoa, man," says Ralph. "Like three ways is cool."

"Forty percent," says Cody. "My equipment and my time—forty percent."

Doug nods at Ralph.

"Okay, okay, man," says Ralph. "Forty percent."

"When do we go?" asks Cody.

"We haven't discussed that," says Doug. "I won't have a full weekend off for three weeks, but my shift ends at seven in the morning."

"I crash on weekends, but I boogie during the week at three," says Ralph.

Cody says, "I see a problem."

"What's that?" asks Doug.

"If someone asks what we are doing, what do we say?"

"Can't we just do it?" says Doug.

Cody answers sternly, "Need reason."

"Like what?"

"Boundary disputes, geological, historical, construction."

"Okay, what if we say we're amateur geologists?" asks Doug.

Cody nods. "Maybe work."

Ralph says, "Okay, okay, man, when do we step off?"

They trade glances, each appearing hesitant.

Finally, Doug speaks up. "With the holidays just around the corner, how about right after the first?"

"Okay, by me," says Cody.

Ralph snorts. "Awesome—cool man."

Chapter Twenty

I've never been a bookworm or much for sifting through dusty catalogs, but Kowalski's suggestion seemed logical, considering the few clues we already had. Although going through boxes of records seemed like a Herculean task, he felt confident we'd find something relevant to our case.

"Stan, you're the history buff. Where do we begin?"

"We need to find any boxes marked Flagstaff history."

Bewildered by the assortment of files, I ask. "I've been in a few libraries in my day, but this collection lacks permanence." The lingering pong of stale cigarettes and beer added to my misplaced notion.

"This used to be the old Elks Club building. They used the basement for social gatherings. It's temporary until the city can raise a bond to construct a new library."

"Where was it before it moved here?" I ask, eager to find the elusive local history box as I casually walk through the collection of containers.

Kowalski stops his own search and turns to me. "Jack, be happy you're here doing our research. They condemned the old library and tore it down last year, just before you joined the force. If we'd been doing our investigation there, we may have run into the ghost."

"Ghost?"

"Yeah, the old custodian of the library killed his wife and children, then went to the library and killed himself. Legend has it, his tortured soul haunts ... I mean, haunted the basement."

I had never encountered a ghost in my years of being a cop. The prospect of finally meeting one sparked my interest, but I let the subject drop.

Kowalski lets out an "Ah, ha," and calls me over.

It's not that I hate research—it's the tedium of flipping through page after page, hoping to find something relevant to our case. My boredom was magnified because neither Kowalski nor I knew what we were looking for. It's one of those things that we would know when we saw it. We found four Bankers Box® containers of information related to Flagstaff's history in some form or another. We started with one box each and began leafing through the files.

About an hour into our search, Kowalski exclaims, "Look what I've found."

Hoping whatever it was would end this mind-numbing hunt, I willingly set aside my stack of history to join him.

I ask, "What's so interesting?"

Like a proud father eager to show off a picture of his newborn child, Kowalski arranges a series of photographs on top of a nearby shelf.

"Have a look at these," he says. "Do you see a familiar face?"

There are seven black and white photographs, with only three with people.

I give them the once over, then, at his prodding, look at them again.

Frustrated by my lack of recognition, he finally says, "The guy in the check shirt—look at him."

I examine them again, paying closer attention to the man in the checkered shirt.

"He looks familiar. I can't ... hey, isn't that Jackson?"

"You bet—younger and a bit leaner," says Kowalski.

I ask, "What does it say on the back of the pictures?"

Kowalski flips them over. "Nothing, except 'I-40 Bridge - 1966.'"

"Yeah, you're right," says Kowalski. "And the snow on the ground gives us some indication of the season."

When it came to local history, Kowalski was at his best. Even though he was a transplant from Milwaukee, listening to him talk about Flagstaff left you with the impression he was a native. Frankly, it's tough working with a know-it-all. I'm glad I'm not like that.

He pulls out another file with the flourish of a carnival barker. "Jack, look at this list. What do you see?"

At first glance, I failed to see anything significant but a list of dates, miles, and locations. Then 1966 popped off the page. "Yeah, I see it. Those pictures and the year correspond to—"

"Canyon Diablo Bridge!" says Kowalski.

"All this stuff has to do with that bridge. But what?" I ask.

"Treasure, Jack—treasure."

Chapter Twenty-One

Kowalski pins three of the seven black-and-white photographs onto our status board, steps back, and says, "Jack, I know it isn't much, but we've added another layer to our investigation."

I was about to give him a word of encouragement when Emily Ruger pops in to pay us a visit.

"There you boys are. I've been looking for you two all morning."

"We were at the old Elks Club building. What's up?" says Kowalski.

"We got an ID on Sam Jackson. His real name is Oscar Eugene Burrows."

"Anything else?" I ask.

She smiles. "You bet. He was a guest of the Northern Correctional Center in Carson City, Nevada."

I ask, "And the charge?"

"Armed robbery," says Ruger. "That was back in 1966—sentenced to fifteen years, but released last year after serving fourteen for good behavior."

She continues to have that, *I know-something smile.*

I say, "I have a feeling you're holding back on us."

She laughs. "Yep. The real kicker is his cellmate. His name is Paul

Grendon, and his specialty was safecracking. They released him three months ago."

Like a dealer laying out the winning card on a royal flush, she pulls a photograph from a manila folder she held by her side. With the alacrity of a card shark, she deposits a prison photo of Grendon on my desk.

Kowalski picks up the eight-by-ten glossy print and pins it to the board. "Doesn't he look like the guy Phyllis Logan described?"

I nod. "It sure does. Now, our web of suspects includes two helpful clues."

"And," says Ruger, once more holding our interest in anticipation of another revelation.

I focus my attention on the folder.

Once more, Ruger pulls out a sheet of paper and waves it in the air. "This is a FAX copy of Jackson's prison record, aka. Oscar Eugene Burrows."

She hands it to me. I give it the once-over—dates, reason for incarceration, education, religion, and occupational skills. As a high school grad, I found his occupational skill—land surveyor—most interesting. I give it to Kowalski.

Kowalski instantaneously picks up on the profession. "What kind of person pulls an armed robbery with that skill and education going for him?"

I say, "A desperate one. Something happened to him in 1966 that may have required a large amount of money."

"It could be anything," says Kowalski. "Medical, gambling debt, or—"

"Grubstake," I interject. "Look, he's at an I-40 construction site in 1966. His record—it's clean except for the robbery. Now he suddenly needs some cash, not necessarily a lot of cash, just enough."

Caught in the moment, I lose track of time and glance at my watch. "Ah, I have to get going. I have to meet someone."

Kowalski gives me his—*what's this all about look*?

Aware of his curiosity, I say, "I'll explain when I see you tomorrow."

Chapter Twenty-Two

The Weatherford Hotel was a quick drive from the Flagstaff police station, and last week's snowfall wasn't a hindrance. I found Jessica sitting alone at the rear of the hotel's only pub, the Charly's Pub and Grill. She looked forlorn, which was understandable considering her situation. She greeted me with a forced smile.

"You're late," she says, not in an accusatory tone, but one of relief. "I thought you might have forgotten."

I pull out a chair and sit across from her. "Were you waiting long?"

"No. Maybe fifteen minutes—just enough time to finish this scotch and soda."

I glance at her drink, which is next to her hotel key. "Want a refill?"

"Sure, I'm not driving."

I motion toward the waitress.

"Speaking of travel, how are you returning to New York?"

"We thought about flying here, but we'd have to take a commuter flight from Phoenix. It was too much of a hassle. Instead, Babs and I decided to make this a train adventure. The train station is a few blocks away, and it's only a couple of days' trip through Chicago. Besides, I rather enjoyed the leisurely trip here. We spent much of our time in the dome car."

The rapid recitation of her travel plans belied her real emotional state.

"How are you feeling?" I ask, looking for any signs that she may break down.

"Actually, Jack, I'm numb. Right now, it's the fear of the unknown that keeps me up at night." She forces a smile.

The waitress arrives, and I order. "One scotch and soda and one neat."

Once we are alone, I ask, "When do you start treatment?"

Fiddling with the hotel's key fob, she hesitates, then says, "A week after I return to New York."

I knew she was searching for my reassurance that all would be okay, but I didn't know what the prognosis was other than her revelation that she had breast cancer. We had been married for twenty years, sufficient time to understand her. She would buy something very expensive, agonize over the cost, and then seek my approval afterward. Now, it was a life-and-death situation, and I honestly couldn't give her that reassurance.

"Did your doctor give you any options regarding your treatments?"

The waitress returns with our order and says, "Continue to charge it to your room, ma'am?"

I raise my hand. "No, I'll pick up the tab on my way out."

"Yes, sir," says the waitress, then turns to leave.

"Thanks, Jack." She raises her drink in my direction.

I acknowledge the gesture with my drink. "I'm curious, why did you pick this hotel? From what I understand, the owners are remodeling it, trying to bring it back to its former glory."

She laughs slightly. "It was Babs' idea. She wanted to stay in a hotel that had some history. She heard that Wyatt Earp stayed here."

I joke, "Well, I think he's already checked out."

Jessica forced a laugh again, but I could see a strain in her reaction.

Clearing my throat, I returned to concerns over her treatment. "I'm sorry, I went off track. What about your treatment?"

Jessica took a sip of scotch. She placed the glass back on the table and swirled the contents before answering. "I don't completely understand, but the treatment involves targeted antibodies along with chemo-therapy. I admit I was still reeling from the news, but the doctor told me it had superior remission rates."

"That should give you some peace of mind," I say, thinking it would have been better if I were involved in the initial consultation. Of course, if we were still married, I would have been there.

"My doctor suggested I get involved in a support group. It's a, never mind ... "

I had taken none of my scotch since the waitress brought it to our table, trying to appear focused on her. I found her dismissiveness trou-bling. "That sounds like fantastic advice. Do you plan on working during your treatment?"

She smiles, hiding behind a defensive nod, one that I was only too well acquainted with. "Jack, I'd like to be around people for support."

Detecting the opportunity to oblige her deception, I raise my glass in a salute and take a sip of my drink.

Jessica obliges with a return gesture. She says, "I don't know about you, Jack, but I'm starved. If we stay here, it will be bar food, like burgers or pizza."

"I agree. I learned about the renovating of this place from my part-ner, Stan."

"They only have a few rooms available. Babs and I were lucky enough to have booked a couple of rooms here months ago."

"Stan Kowalski's the historian. I'll have to ask him tomorrow what he knows of this place."

"Babs told me that back in the 1930s, a honeymoon couple got murdered in this hotel."

"Well, that's a crime I won't have to worry about."

Jessica lets out an explosive laugh, the first real one I've seen on her since we met.

"I'll take you to a nice place."

"I'd like that, Jack." She picks up her hotel key and drops it into her purse.

I pay the bar bill, and we leave.

Once in my car, she leans over and kisses me on the cheek.

She says, "I need you, Jack."

The combination of scotch and sadness can wreak havoc on a person's psyche. I knew in the end, I would be shattering her world. But now it was about the moment, and I didn't want to hurt her.

Chapter Twenty-Three

"Where did you go in such a hurry yesterday?" Kowalski asks as I enter our office.

His question was not unexpected. While removing my overcoat, I mull over my answer. Thinking it may be therapeutic to share, I say, "I had dinner with my ex-wife."

Kowalski looks me straight in the eye and says, "Wow! How long has she been in town?"

I let out an uneasy laugh. "Over a week now."

"And you decided to tell me now?"

"Hey, this has been a complete surprise for me, too. I've been trying to digest it."

"She's missing you and comes all this way to have dinner with you?"

I turn toward the clothes rack and hang up my coat. With my back facing Kowalski, I say, "She's got breast cancer."

Turning back, I see Kowalski's face change from a teasing smile to concern.

"How serious is it?" he asks.

Pensively shaking my head, I say, "I don't know all the details. She plans on getting treatment a week after she returns to New York."

"Is that why she came to Flagstaff?"

"She's here with a friend."

"What, a guy?" Kowalski asks in apparent astonishment.

"Nah, it's not like that. She's got this flighty friend called Babs. Her real name is Donna. The two of them came out here for a vacation. That's her excuse, but I think she came out here for support"

"What, you think she wants to get back together?"

"Last night, over dinner, she kinda suggested that."

"So, what did you say?"

"In essence, I told her too much water had gone under the bridge. The divorce had been messy, and I said I didn't think it was possible, considering everything that happened. She wants me to have dinner with her on Christmas Eve, but I told her I already had other plans."

"Hey, Jack, it's all right if you want to have dinner with her instead of with us. Mary will understand, given the circumstances."

"No, Stan, I made a promise to join you and your family, and I'm going to keep it."

"Your call," says Kowalski.

"Besides, she then suggested New Year's Eve. I said okay. Now that we've cleared that up, let's get down to business," I say, pointing toward the murder board.

"Jack, I think we should pay that night clerk another visit. I got the feeling he's hiding something."

"I agree. But I would rather make it a house call to catch him off guard."

Kowalski looks at his watch. "It's early, and he is probably at home right now."

"Hey, Stan, I didn't get my morning cup of coffee yet."

"We'll get one on the way, and I could use a quick breakfast, too," Kowalski says while retrieving my overcoat before handing it to me.

Chapter Twenty-Four

S tanding outside Doug McGuire's apartment, I make out the muffled sounds of a television broadcast.

"Sounds like we're in luck," says Kowalski.

I knock.

From inside, I hear a scurry of activity, and the TV noise goes dead. The door opens, and I see Doug McGuire's face turn white.

Out of routine, I flash my badge even though he recognizes me. "Mr. McGuire, we would like to ask you a few questions. May we come in?"

"Shu ... sure, Detective," he says as he opens the door.

I notice the television. The sound is off, but it appears Doug likes to watch reruns of *All in the Family*.

Dressed in jeans and a white t-shirt but shoeless, Doug aims the remote and turns off the set. He gestures toward the kitchenette. "I'm afraid I don't have a lot of seating options other than the couch."

"The kitchen table is fine by us," I say, and follow Doug.

The table has three mismatched chairs. Doug takes the furthest chair with the stove behind him and the sink on his right. I sit opposite him while Kowalski grabs the chair in the middle.

Wanting my silence to provoke unease, I wait for Doug to speak.

Doug began fiddling with a pencil. Rolling it back and forth on the table, he stops it mid-roll and glances at Kowalski before looking back at me. "Am I in some sort of trouble?"

I say, "Only if you are withholding information."

Kowalski chimes in. "Are you?"

"Hey, I told you guys everything. Jackson checks in late at night and, to the best of my knowledge, goes directly to his room."

Staring at him, he averts my eyes. "And that's it?"

"Yeah, the next thing I heard about him was the following day."

Wishing for a confession, I press, "Didn't that surprise you?"

"Well, yeah, anytime someone dies in our hotel, it's a shock."

I reply, "How many have died at the Double Six Hotel?"

Doug squirms and shrugs. "Since I've been there?"

"Yeah."

"Including Jackson?"

"Yep, go on."

"Three. I think the other two were heart attacks."

"Okay. Now, the desk clerk, Phyllis Logan, says a man came in during her shift and asked about Mr. Jackson. Do you know anything about that?" I ask.

He vigorously shakes his head. "No. Phyllis told me about him and told me she gave him my name. That's all I know."

"Did anyone come here or visit you at work concerning Mr. Jackson's death?"

Licking his lips, he shook his head. "No."

Kowalski says, "Did you talk to anyone about the death?"

Looking at Kowalski, I see color rising to Doug's cheeks. "Aha, ... just to my friend, Ralph Tyler."

"So, what does your friend do for a living?"

"He works for the city."

Feeling like I'm pulling teeth, I ask, "What does he do for the city?"

"He's a trash collector."

Kowalski and I trade glances.

I ask, "What did you tell him?"

"Nothing much. What's there to tell? The guy comes in and give... I mean, he gave me his name and paid for the room." He shrugs. "Then he gets killed. That's all I know, and that's all I told Ralph."

"We've taken enough of your time." I ask, "Do you have your friend's address?

Hesitantly, he reaches for the pencil and rips off a piece of paper from a nearby notepad. As he writes, the tip of the pencil breaks. Appearing frustrated, he looks at me for support.

Kowalski hands him his ballpoint pen.

With a less-than-steady hand, he scribbles out the address. Laying the pen on the note, he slides it toward Kowalski.

Kowalski retrieves both items and places them in the breast pocket of his coat. We both rise, exchange handshakes, and turn to leave.

Doug follows us to the door, but before we reach it, he says, "Ralph doesn't get home until after three."

Kowalski glanced at his watch. "Thanks. That saves us a trip."

Even without the update, I knew we were in for a long afternoon.

Chapter Twenty-Five

"The key. Did you notice the key on the table?" I ask Kowalski as we approach our car.

He unlocks the driver's side and says over the car's roof, "I can't say I did. His table had a lot of junk on it. What of it?"

I waited until he unlocked my door. I slipped into the passenger side. "It was an old key with a very distinctive shape. But the real mystery for me, anyway, was my ex-wife having a similar key from the Weatherford Hotel. To the best of my knowledge, there isn't any connection between the two of them."

"Okay, so it's obvious what we need to do. Right, Jack?"

"Yeah, let's pop in at the Weatherford and at least satisfy my curiosity."

Kowalski starts the ignition, and even before our heater warms the interior, places the car in gear and exits Doug McGuire's parking lot.

* * *

Like most of Flagstaff, the Weatherford glowed in its Christmas finery. At street level, it was illuminated with a dazzling display of white fairy lights, which gave me the impression that the building was about to levitate to the heavens.

"Pretty nice, hey Stan?" I say as my eyes travel to the top of the structure, where a lighted Christmas tree serves as a showy climax.

"Yeah, they put on a nice display for the holidays. I understand the owner plans on replacing the balcony."

"Not to kill the mood, Stan, by the looks of the crowded streets, we may have a hard time finding parking."

Kowalski laughs. "Trust me, we'll find a spot out back."

* * *

The sign on the door says, "No vacancy." Considering the season, that didn't surprise me. The middle-aged woman behind the counter wore a burgundy outfit from the twentieth century, matching the hotel's historical era. The dress was full-sleeved, with a V-shaped front of white lace, accented by a floral embroidery trim at the bodice. She was leaning over and engrossed, I assumed, in hotel-related paperwork. Reacting to the tinkle of the door's suspended bell, she looks up.

She says, "Good evening, and merry Christmas," with a smile, even before the sun had barely begun to cast its shadow.

"Good evening and merry Christmas. I'm Detective Owens, and this is Detective Kowalski."

Kowalski displays his shield.

"Is there some problem?" she asks, her face exhibiting concern.

I reply, "We are investigating the recent murder in the Double Six Hotel."

Her look of apprehension turns to bewilderment. "How does that concern us?"

"Frankly, at this point," I began, "I'm not sure, but I have a question for you that may shed some light on the case."

"I'm Jean, the assistant manager, but maybe you would rather speak with the owner. What do you need?"

"No," I say. "I'm certain you can answer my questions. First, I would like to look at one of your room keys."

"Our keys?" Jean asks probingly.

"Yes, please."

She pulls out a drawer, removes a key with its attached fob, and hands it to me. An expression of puzzlement remains on her face. Without us asking, she hauls out another key, only this one is blank.

Kowalski picks it up and jokes, "I bet you have a hard time keeping these in stock?"

Jean laughs. "We did until we put a deposit fee on them. We still have a few that fail to return them—mostly honeymoon couples."

I ask, "How many blanks do you have?"

"Oh, probably a hundred ... more or less. What I've been told is that there used to be a locksmith next door to the barbershop around the corner. He just moved into town and set up his business. I think he started with this hotel. I understand he later got gold fever and went north to the Yukon. He put up his entire inventory for sale. I understand the owner back then thought it advantageous to have a lot of extras."

"That's an interesting story," says Kowalski, sliding back his key to Jean. "How many rooms do you have?"

"I was told that it originally had 42 rooms, but that was back in 1900. Those were the days when a bed and a private place to sleep were all that a traveler needed. Nowadays, people want their own bathroom, with a shower, a big bed, and a television."

I ask, "How many rooms do you have now?"

"Back in 1975, when remodeling began, we had twelve with plans on increasing that number to seventeen."

"Well, Jean, I believe we have all the information we need," I say, handing back the key. I hesitate. "Do you suppose we could borrow that blank key?"

She shrugged. "I don't see the problem." She reached for the blank and then slid it toward me.

After saying our goodbyes, we move toward the entrance and pause. I say, "Tomorrow is Christmas Eve. I'd like to put this part of the investigation to bed. Let's take a trip back to Doug McGuire's place and see his reaction when I show him our key."

Chapter Twenty-Six

Expecting the detectives to be in wait outside Ralph's trailer, Doug panics and dresses for the cold weather with the speed of a fireman. Pausing in mid-retreat, he lifts one of the metal slats on his window blinds and sneaks a peek outside. Seeing nothing of concern, he turns away, leaving the blind askew, then goes to finish dressing.

Doug starts his Pacer and waits until the interior is warm before he puts it in gear. With the frequency of a getaway driver, his eyes dart ahead for any sign of danger. As careful as he is, the holiday traffic hinders his ability to be certain he isn't being followed.

Using up most of an hour, Doug finally finds Ralph behind the wheel of a Flagstaff garbage truck. He blows the horn, and Ralph returns the greeting with a boisterous blast from his own horn. Doug pulls two car lengths ahead of the truck and stops. Leaving the Pacer idle, he jumps out of the car and runs up to the driver's side of the truck.

Ralph rolls down his window. "Hey, man, wazup?" he shouts down to Doug over the rumble of the truck's engine.

"Ralph, when you're done with work, come straight to my place. Got that?"

"Hey, you're the man," he says and gives him a shoddy hand salute.

The two members of the sanitation crew advance from behind the truck and gawk forward.

Doug waves back and charges toward his car.

With that out of the way, he retraces his route home. Even with the cold weather, his hands are moist against the steering wheel with a white-knuckled grip while his mind races for solutions. He knows he is too far into the mess he created to come clean, and the prospect of wealth motivates him not to change course. He thinks *I could deny everything because my connection to it was dead. The only evidence linking me was the envelope with its hidden secrets. Because of its potential to make me rich, I can't destroy it. I need to hide it ...*

He hits the brake pedal. *Ralph ... I hafta go back to talk with him.*

Doug checks for traffic before making a U-turn. Now, it's a race against time to find Ralph. He knew Ralph might be heading toward the dump. Doug heads to the last place he talked to Ralph. Finally reaching his first encounter with him, Doug follows the path of empty and a few dumped-over garbage cans. The trail ends on the outskirts of town. With his stomach churning, Doug stomps on the gas pedal. Heading north on Highway 89, he hopes to catch up to Ralph before he turns onto Landfill Road. In the distance, he glimpses Ralph's truck.

When Doug catches up to Ralph, he pounds on the horn and flashes his lights to get him to pull over. As Ralph slows down, Doug passes him and comes to a stop on the shoulder of the highway.

Not waiting for Ralph to come to a full stop, Doug jumps out of his AMC Pacer and runs toward the moving truck. The dump truck's brakes squeal as it comes to a stop. The truck door opens, and Ralph climbs down to meet Doug.

"Hey man," says Ralph. "What's crackin'? I already told you I'd come to your pad after work."

Breathing heavily, Doug coughs out, "The cops ... they may ... be waiting for you ... when you punch out."

"What's the man want to see me for?"

"They came to my place and began questioning me about that Jackson guy. They asked me if I had told anyone about the murder. I said I told you."

"So what?"

"I think, they think we know more than we I'm telling them."

"No problemo, man," says Ralph.

"Okay, okay, good. Remember, I just told you about the murder, that's all."

"Take a chill pill, man. I got you covered."

"Thanks."

"Hey man, I gotta book it. Catch you on the flip side."

Chapter Twenty-Seven

As Doug drives home, his mind becomes preoccupied with hiding the envelope and Ralph's faithfulness to his promise of confidentiality, even in the face of police questioning. Those thoughts were unrelenting as he climbed the stairs to his apartment. Those contemplations give way to other concerns, like doubting his ability to function with only three hours of sleep before assuming his night shift at the Double Six Hotel.

Closing the door behind him, he thought he heard someone climbing the steps. *It's too early for Ralph. The police? It can't be the police again?*

He removed his coat and tossed it onto the sofa. He then walked toward the bathroom until he heard a knock on the door. With hesitant steps, he turned back and warily unfastened the latch.

Greeted by a tall man dressed in a weathered brown leather bomber jacket, which contrasted with his newer wide-brim hat, pristine jeans, and scuffed Bowie boots, Doug keeps a firm grip on the doorknob.

"Hi, I'm Paul Grendon. I understand you are the clerk at the Double Six Hotel."

"Yeah, what of it?" says Doug, his eyes darting from side to side, thinking the man may have a friend.

"I understand you were the person who checked in Sam Jackson a few nights ago."

"Yeah."

"I just need a moment of your time."

"I have nothing to say."

The man remains persistent. "Phyllis, your co-worker, told me the police questioned you."

"I don't know you. I told the police that he checked in, went directly to his room, and that was the last I heard of him—that is, of course, until the next day when I found out he died."

"There may be more you have overlooked. If you can let me in—"

"Listen, mister, I've got to get some sleep. I told you everything I know. Goodbye," says Doug before slamming the door.

Doug's heart pounds as he listens to the sound of retreating steps. He goes to the window, spots the gap left from before in the metal blinds, and peeks out to see the man get into his car and leave. Doug breaths a sigh of relief.

With the man gone, Doug flips on his coat without zippering it and heads down to his car. He approaches it from the passenger side then unlocks the car door. Without hesitation, he opens the glove compartment and retrieves his Harrington & Richardson .22 caliber revolver. Shuffling it into an inside coat pocket, he hurriedly makes his way back to his apartment.

Once Doug finished shaving and showering, he expected Ralph to have arrived by now. Glancing at his watch countless times only added to his anxiety. *Did he crack under police questioning? Are the police on their way to arrest him? Doug lay on his couch, wanting to sleep, but doubted he would.*

Reaching that sweet zone where anxiety surrenders to slumber, Doug jolted awake upon hearing the knocking at his door. Unlike the tale of *The Lady or the Tiger, Doug only had one door to open* and was bound to whatever fate greeted him. He glances at his watch and was surprised he had slept for nearly two hours. *Was Ralph questioned by the police for all this time?* He rolled off the couch when another knock once more broke the silence.

"I'm coming," he shouts and shuffles his way to the door.

Doug's pounding heart skips a beat when he sees Ralph's smiling face.

"The police questioned you this whole time?" he asks and strolls in out of the cold without an invitation.

Ralph shakes off the few snowflakes from his jacket before going to the kitchen, where he drapes his coat over one of the chairs. "Nah, Five-O never showed. My battery died on me. What a nightmare. I had to get a jump and then find a store. Okay, give me the lowdown on why you're freakin' out."

Doug, outfitted in jeans and a sweatshirt, joins Ralph and sits down opposite him at the table. "I'm just surprised the cops didn't question you at work."

"Did they say they were going to?"

"No, I just thought—"

The knock on Doug's apartment door made both of the men look at each other with surprise.

"Maybe that's them now?" says Ralph.

"Just be cool, Ralph. Let me do most of the talking," Doug says, making his way toward the unknown night caller.

Upon opening the door and without the benefit of a mirror, Doug knew his face had turned white. It wasn't only seeing Paul Grendon that worried him; it was the gun in his hand that concerned him the most.

Chapter Twenty-Eight

Starting out on our way to Doug McGuire's place, we sat in silence for a couple of miles. My detachment centered on Jessica's medical condition. Knowing Kowalski's moods, I suspect his involved visions of sugarplums dancing in his head—that's what happens when you are a father at Christmas time. Although Kowalski was senior to me in the Flagstaff Police Department, he generally deferred to my judgment. In the beginning, I wondered whether his acquiescent nature was inherent or calculating, letting me assume something that would be my undoing. I guess my background as a New York City cop made me more skeptical of people. It didn't take me too long to realize he was the real deal—genuinely considerate.

Kowalski broke the silence. "Jack, you are still coming to Christmas dinner?"

"The only other option I had was your place or a Hungry-Man meal."

"They still make them?" asks Kowalski.

"Rub it in, Stan. You've been away from the single life for so long that you forgot the hardships that came along with that lifestyle."

"Yep, and thinking of lifestyles, I feel sorry for that McGuire kid.

Yeah, I remember those days. Not only is he trying to make his way in life, but he gets a gut-punch with the divorce."

"Yeah, the divorce," I agree. "I'm looking at this case through the eyes of someone who has money problems. Stan, I think he's holding back on us."

"Like what?"

"I'm puzzled. My New York City cop's intuition tells me he's keeping something from us."

"What would he have to gain?" asks Kowalski.

"I'm thinking more of what he would have to lose. Maybe Jackson gave him some information that has a monetary value."

Kowalski scoffs, "Like who's going to win the Super Bowl, the Pittsburgh Steelers, or the Los Angeles Rams?"

"Yeah, wouldn't we all want to know that?"

"Well, we're here, Jack. You can ask him yourself."

"That's what I plan on doing, Stan. Just maybe we'll solve this case by New Year's Eve."

We both laugh and exit the car.

Kowalski took the lead and began climbing the stairs. When we reached the top, I noticed his labored breathing. "Are you okay?" I ask, concerned because his behavior was unusual.

He took in a breath and says, "I'm okay. I think it's all the holiday stress."

Still troubled by his less-than-convincing answer, I say, "Maybe you'd better let me do all the talking."

"Jack, I'm fine. If anything, I'm a bit tired, that's all."

As I approach Doug McGuire's place, I take a peek through a crooked blind and see a man holding a gun. I draw my weapon.

"What's up?" asks Kowalski.

In a lowered voice, I say, "We have an armed man holding a gun on McGuire and another man."

I knock forcefully.

I hear a flurry of movement from the other side. With my gun drawn and pointed at the ready, I brace myself for the expected confrontation.

As the door opens, I push forward and yell, "Freeze!"

Doug McGuire totters backward and falls. I see the other man hit the floor, but the armed man is no longer present.

Looking down at McGuire, I demand, "Where the hell is the guy with the gun?"

In a daze of apparent confusion, he points toward the bathroom.

Moving to my left, I glance over my right shoulder to check Kowalski's position. To my surprise, his gun was still holstered. Instead, he was bent over and seemingly in pain.

"McGuire, get up and call 911!"

While he staggered to the kitchen phone, I continued to the bathroom. "Mister! Throw out your weapon and come out with your hands in the air."

I repositioned myself to the right, knowing he would not have a clear view of me until the door was at least halfway open.

I hear McGuire make the phone call unsteadily.

I yell, "Throw out your weapon!"

McGuire cradles the phone. From his crouched-down position under the kitchen table, he shouts, "There's a window in the bathroom."

Now realizing the stranger may have left, I stand to the side of the doorway. I grab the doorknob, twist it, and push. As the door slams against the wall, I turn into the open doorframe. My revolver swiftly scans the interior. The glow from the outside street lamps lights the bathroom while a rush of cold air hurries past me. The open window gives evidence that the night intruder is gone. Moving to the window, I look down and see the indentation in the snowbank. With Kowalski's health condition and the time lost, I reason the pursuit was pointless. The cry of an approaching ambulance grows.

Chapter Twenty-Nine

Doug sat at his kitchen table in silence. Ralph kept looking at him from across the table as if to get directions on what he would say after the ambulance left. Doug, with barely a discernible effort, shook his head and mouthed, *say nothing.*

When the ambulance left, instead of feeling at ease, Doug felt a foreboding. As Detective Owens closed the door and turned toward him, his stomach burned with a surge of acid. He approaches the kitchen nook, removes the phone from the wall, and then dials a number. He turns away from them and moves as far as the coiled cord would allow.

Even with a hushed voice, Doug understood the gist of the conversation. Finished, he assured the person at the other end that he would meet them at the hospital. Somber-faced, Owens looked uneasy.

Inspector Owens takes the center chair and sits down. Resting his hands on the table, he shifts his gaze between Doug and Ralph. "The reason we came here was to ask you a few questions. I had no idea we were going into a buzz-saw. Now, why was that man here, and why did he have a gun trained on you?"

Doug felt intimidated, and the only word that came out of his mouth was, "Ahh."

"Listen, cut the bullshit and hemming and hawing. I have to go to the hospital. Now, why was he here?"

Ralph squirmed in place and gave Doug an unspoken plea with his eyes.

"Okay, that man, I forgot his name, came here earlier. He asked me if that Jackson fella said or gave me something when he checked into the hotel."

"And what did you tell him?"

"I said he didn't say, do, or give me anything."

"Obviously, he thinks differently."

"Listen, Detective, I don't have a clue what he thinks, and our exchange involved me checking him into the hotel. That's it."

Detective Owens turns toward Ralph. "Is he telling the truth?"

Ralph jerks back. "Hey, man, that's all I know is what he just told you. That's the skinny. We only chill."

"One more thing," Inspector Owens says and points toward the key on the table. "Where did you get that key?"

"Um ..., I found it in one of our hotel rooms a while back. It was unusual. That's why I hung on to it."

"Do you have any idea where it came from?" Owens asks.

"No. Like I said, I thought it was unusual, and that's why I kept it."

"Well, for your information, it belongs to the Weatherford Hotel."

Doug felt a surge of adrenaline rush through his body. He says, "Wow." His own voiced exclamation took him by surprise; it was his subconscious response overwhelming his passive compliance. Now he hoped his reaction didn't betray him for Owens to make more of it than a simple flash of surprise. His palms sweat.

Unfazed, Owes gets up. "I have to go. If that man contacts you again, call me right away."

Both Doug and Ralph sit mute.

"Do you understand?" Owens says, his tone suggesting frustration.

"Yes," Doug and Ralph say in unison.

"I'll see myself out," Owens mumbles, then heads for the door.

As if glued to their seats, Doug and Ralph stay put until he leaves the apartment.

Chapter Thirty

The door to Doug's apartment slams. Ralph is about to say something, but Doug warns him with a forceful shake of his head. "Not now," he whispers, then waits with bated breath.

Using extreme caution, Doug rises and makes his way to the window. He carefully peels back the blind to take a peek. Although it appears that Detective Owens is gone, Doug isn't relieved.

He turns back to Ralph. Like a spring that reached its breaking point unleashes a torrent of expletives and says, "Shit, shit, shit, and double shit."

Ralph's eyes widen. "Hey, man, what are we gonna do?"

Doug, his mind reeling with confusion, joins Ralph and began pacing. "Everything was going fine until that jerk showed up with a gun."

"Are we gonna hafta spill the beans to Five-O?"

"At this point, we can't. If we talk, we risk going to jail for obstruction ... and maybe even an accomplice to murder."

"Murder?" asks Ralph.

"Shit. I haven't the foggiest." Doug sits down on the middle kitchen chair. He grabs the key from the table. While rubbing the key between his thumb and index finger, he says, "At least we now know more about this key."

"That's good, huh?" says Ralph.

"You bet it is. Puzzled, I wondered about its significance and what it opened. Now I know. My guess is that it opens room 209."

"Okay, so it opens room 209. So what?"

"So, I don't know. Maybe whoever got involved in this buried treasure stuff forgot to give back the key after staying there. I know from school that the hotel was built sometime around 1897."

"So?"

"So, the big train robbery occurred in 1889. That's a difference of eight years."

"I don't get it," says Ralph.

"Whoever is involved with the treasure map happened way after the robbery. I'm thinking someone accidentally found the treasure and, for some reason, marked its location so they could come back later."

"And?"

"Ralph, that's the $64,000 question."

"What about Cody?" asks Ralph.

"We'll keep it between the two of us. It may spook him if he hears about that guy with a gun."

"I'll do a Bogart."

"Bogart?"

"Yeah, like, keep to myself," says Ralph, rising from his chair. "Hey, I gotta book—work tomorrow."

"Yep, me too. I'll be lucky if I can get an hour of sleep before I check in. Ahh ..., Ralph, before you go, there's one more thing."

"What's that kemo sahbee?"

"You still got your shotgun?"

"Yeah."

"Considering what's all going down—keep it handy."

"Ten-four."

Chapter Thirty-One

Emily Ruger stands in the break room, holding a cup of coffee while staring out the window. The room is empty except for the two of us.

"You're early, too," I say, making my way toward the coffee urn.

"Yeah, when did you get the news about Kowalski?" I ask.

"It was about nine last night, right around the time I usually go to bed."

"That's kinda early isn't it to go to bed?"

"I read. It helps me sleep. Unfortunately, last night's news did little for me in that category."

"Yeah, me too. Even a double scotch didn't help either." I grab my standby cup, the one I use when I skip my favorite coffee shop's brew.

"I don't drink," she replies with conviction. "Did the Chief call you, too, last night?"

"No, I guess he figured I already knew what happened." I began filling my cup.

"Well, I wish he had. It would have saved me this awkward position of telling you I'm your new partner."

"Shit," I snap, upset with my aim and equally stunned by the news.

"Honestly, I really wasn't expecting that kind of reaction."

I place my cup on the counter and grab a paper towel. Stooping down to wipe off the spilled coffee from my shoes, I say, "No, it wasn't that, it was my unsteady hand."

"I probably should have told you after you finished pouring your coffee."

"Nah," I say. "If you had waited, it would have been my tie and shirt rather than my shoes."

We both laugh.

Feeling a bit more at ease, I took a sip of coffee. "This coffee isn't half bad."

"Thank you for your backhanded compliment," says Emily while raising her cup toward me in a salute.

"You made it?"

"Yep. I thought I'd give the outgoing shift a break and make the coffee. Tea is my favorite, but occasionally I have a cup or two."

I joke, "Be careful, you may have a new job."

She makes her way to the break room table, pulls out a chair, and sits. I follow and sit across from her. We each set our cups down in front of us.

Her demeanor gave me the feeling, acquired through years of ritual as a married man, that I was in for a lecture. And my sixth sense proved correct as soon as she opened her mouth.

"John," she begins with a lingering hold on my name, the same way my wife Jessica held fast to it before dropping a bomb.

Trained as I was as an obedient husband, I say, "Yes." *I leave out the dear since we were not at that level of familiarity.*

"I don't know what you and Kowalski talked about when you guys shoot the breeze, but I would like to establish some ground rules."

I took a measured sip of my coffee while Emily tested hers.

To your question, we talk about knitting, baking, and what we are going to do when we grow up. But, I digress. "Go on."

"First, I don't care for any off-color jokes."

Oh, I'm glad you told me that. I had a real humdinger. I nod.

"When we're among our peers, we should keep it professional, like sergeant and detective."

Too bad. I was thinking of calling you toots. I nod.

"And finally, no fraternization after work hours."

So much for me asking you out on a date, lady. I nod again.

She says, "You've done a lot of nodding. Any questions?"

"Nope, everything is fine, and I completely understand. No jokes and no socializing. Got it."

"Well, I didn't mean no fun, I meant ... ."

Our eyes met, and I began to smirk.

"Never mind," she snaps. "I think you get the picture. It's your turn."

"Everything you said was exactly what I was going to say. So, I think we'll get along just fine."

She looked as if she was about to burst out laughing, but seemed to contain herself.

"Now that we have established the ground rules of our relationship, let's talk about the case Kowalski and I were on."

"I think I know the gist of it."

"Here's something you don't know. The reason Kowalski and I went to see that hotel clerk, Doug McGuire, was to question him about a key."

"That's important—how?"

"When I had dinner with my ex-wife, I noticed the key to her hotel room."

"Your ex lives here?" Emily asks, apparently surprised.

"No, she's here on vacation. A long story."

The frequency of our sips increased as our coffee became more tepid.

With a bit of awkward nuance, she asks, "What's so special about a key?"

"In a previous visit to McGuire's place, I noticed he had the same style key. It, too, had a stamp with the manufacturer's name, Francis Keil & Sons. I asked him where he got it."

"And his answer?"

"The predictable reply of criminals going back to grade school is, 'I found it.'"

"So, you think it has something to do with the case?"

"Yes, and I noted the number 209 stamped into it."

"So, is that where we are going this morning?"

"It's Christmas Eve. We can wait a couple of days before we call on the Weatherford Hotel. Unless we get another murder, consider the following few days' holidays.

Chapter Thirty-Two

I stand outside the door to Jessica's hotel room. I have to admit that I was nervous and had second thoughts. Finally, I knock, hoping she might have left for dinner with Babs. A stirring of activity from inside was followed by the unbolting of the lock.

"John? What brings you here? Did the hotel manager call the police because of the loud television noise?"

I couldn't help but laugh. "Yeah. I'm going to have to take you out for dinner."

"If that's the punishment for breaking the law in Flagstaff, I just might consider staying. Before I commit myself to self-incrimination without hearing my Miranda rights, I thought you had a prior engagement."

"If you let me in, I'll tell you the whole story."

"Of course. Come in, Jack. I wasn't expecting company, and my bed is in a mess because I wanted to get a jump on packing." She points toward the desk chair. "Seating's limited. Why don't you sit over there, and I'll sit here on the bed."

After getting situated, I begin, "Kowalski and I were making our last call of the day, and after climbing a flight of stairs, he collapsed."

"My goodness. Is he ...."

"No, he got lucky, but I think he won't be working with me for a while." I add, "Maybe for a really long time. Anyway, as you know, I had been invited to his house for dinner and ... . Well, here I am asking if you would join me for dinner?"

"As you can see, Jack, I'm not really dressed for dinner, but I appreciate the thought."

"By the way, where is Babs?"

"You know, Babs, Jack. She is one of those rare individuals who can fall in love at the drop of a hat."

I laugh. "Yep, no need to explain." I scan the floor before looking up at her. "Listen, Jessica, you look fine. I'll wait in the hotel lobby and give you a few minutes to get ready. No excuses. Okay?"

At that moment, I saw the woman I fell in love with return. Her warm smile reminded me of happier days. "Always the charmer, Jack. I'll see you in the lobby."

* * *

When I walked in, the lobby was empty. The hotel's reception desk was hidden from view but nestled to my right under a staircase. Turning, I found a pretty girl behind the counter who greeted me with a pleasant smile. Like Jean, the assistant manager, she wore a period outfit, although not as elaborate. Her long-sleeved light blue dress, with its modest neckline trimmed in black velvet, matched her cuffs and wrapped up with a sash around her waist.

I greet her, "Merry Christmas."

"Merry Christmas to you, too, sir. How may I help you?"

"I'm fine, thank you. I'm waiting for a guest at your hotel. She told me she would be down in a few minutes, but I think it may take a bit longer." I laugh.

She also laughs, sharing my skepticism. "Yes, sir. We women need a bit more time."

A nagging question in my head has plagued me since I was here last. "I'm curious about this hotel."

"Sir?"

"I was here earlier and talked with Jean, your assistant manager. I'm

Detective Jack Owens from the Flagstaff Police Department. I hate to mix business with pleasure, but I have a question."

She looked at me quizzically. "I don't know if I can help, but what's your question?"

"At one time, I understand this hotel had 42 rooms."

"Uh-huh, that's what I heard, too. Of course, that was before television and private baths." She laughs.

"Do you, by any chance, have seen old building layouts or architectural drawings of this hotel?"

Her pleasant demeanor expanded with a broad smile. "Besides my employment here, I also work at the Lowell Observatory. I'm working to save enough money to go to the University of Arizona in Tucson. I have a keen interest in the sciences and history."

I was getting a little impatient and wasn't interested in her life's story. "And?"

"Oh. The reason I mentioned that is architecture is also one of my interests. I found the original drawing of this hotel fascinating."

"And where did you see them?"

"In the office on the second floor. The owner has them in frames."

Chapter Thirty-Three

"Wow, what a knockout," my knee-jerk reaction to Jessica as she strolls down the staircase into the lobby. She wore one of those little black dresses that proved to be an ambush for many unsuspecting men. My eyes travel to the plunging neckline.

She smiles. Even in the dimly lit room, I could see a definite blush rise to her face. "So, where are you going to take me in one of the most difficult times of the year to find an open restaurant?"

She hands me her black coat. By its weight, I could tell it wasn't sufficient to shield her from Flagstaff's chill. I help her put it on.

"Winslow," I say.

"I never heard of Winslow. Is it far?"

I ignore the question. "A few months after arriving in Flagstaff, I made my acquaintance with a restaurant owner in Winslow. I called him while you were getting ready, and he said, 'Come on over—the more, the merrier.'"

"'The more, the merrier?'" quizzes Jessica, her face wrinkling up.

During our short walk to my car, we pass several couples who were exuberantly embracing the holiday season. Despite Kowalski's illness and active murder case, I, too, was in a festive mood while exchanging greetings in passing. I could see Jessica also allowed herself to be swept up in the moment.

I open the car door for her.

She looks up at me with an entreating smile, but my guard was up, and it failed to engulf me.

I move to the driver's side and get in. As I start the car, I say, "This place is closed because of Christmas Eve."

"And he was so taken by your charm that he now considers you part of the family?"

Jessica still had that tinge of sarcasm that cancer couldn't defeat. I laugh. "No. It was one of those matters of fate. I was driving back from Holbrook when I came upon a car stalled alongside the highway. The man in the car was Pete Pairopoulos, a co-owner of the Pindos Palace Restaurant. Long story short, we hit it off and became friends. Anytime I was in the neighborhood, I would make it a point to stop in for a visit."

"Pairopoulos? The name sounds Greek."

"How about Mexican?" I say with a smile.

"You mean the name or the food?"

"The food, my dear. You'll love it. Pete thought more people in these parts would be interested in Mexican food than Greek."

"'My dear?'" I'm not sure if you ever called me that."

Wishing I had not invoked the persona of Clark Gable, I disregard her remark and say, "Get comfortable, Winslow's a bit of a ride."

Her comeback was instantaneous. It was as if she had prepped herself, waiting for the right moment. "That just gives us that much more time to get reacquainted," she says, her remark reminiscent of some movie I couldn't place yet in the annals of Hollywood, but sure it existed.

Now that I had committed myself, I began to have second thoughts. I pressed down on the accelerator and primed myself for discussion.

* * *

As parties go, our Christmas sojourn turned out to be one for the record books. My assumption of Mexican fare proved mistaken. Instead, we enjoyed *moussaka*, *souvlaki*, and *choriatiki*, for starters, and that was only some of what I could remember. The deserts, too, were plentiful. From my favorite *baklava* to *loukoumades* and treats, I couldn't remember.

"Tired?" I ask.

"Who wouldn't be with all the Greek food, music, and dancing?" Jessica admitted.

"I knew we had a trip ahead of us. So, I only had one drink of *tsikoudia*."

"Yeah," Jessica says sleepily. "What was that stuff?"

"I think it's homemade."

"I had two," she says, her eyes drooping to the point of near closure. "It's potent stuff."

"Yep, that's why I only had one, knowing we had a trip ahead of us."

"Jack, would you mind if I close my eyes and nap?"

"Jessica, I'm surprised you lasted this long. Sure, go ahead."

"Are you sure you're okay to drive without someone keeping you company?" she asks before dropping off to sleep without waiting for a response.

* * *

"Here we are," I say, lucky enough to find a parking spot in front of the hotel.

She took in a long breath and looks around. "That was fast. Do you want to come up for a cup of coffee?"

"What about Babs?"

"I pretty much had the room to myself during our stay."

"As much as I would like to, it probably isn't a good idea," I say, preparing myself for a chivalrous farewell.

"Jack, I'm glad we had this time together," she says, moving toward me. "It meant a lot to me." She paused. "Jack, one more favor."

"What is it?" I ask, hoping it's something uncomplicated.

"Tomorrow ..." she laughs. "I meant today—I'll be sleeping in and packing later. Do you suppose we could have a late dinner?"

"What about breakfast?" I ask.

"The train leaves at five a.m. You okay with that?"

I smile. "Dinner's fine, providing I'm not involved in anything at the station."

She comes closer and leans forward to kiss me. I reciprocate.

She pulls back and seductively says, "Merry Christmas. Dinner at six?"

Captivated by her charm and holding me in its grasp, I nod and say, "Merry Christmas."

She promptly opens the door and exits. From her position on the sidewalk, she waves, turns toward the hotel, and disappears inside without looking back.

Chapter Thirty-Four

I roll over in bed and see it's still Christmas, although it's Christmas afternoon. With no social engagements to worry about, the day was my own. My first order of business was brewing a pot of coffee, followed by a wake-me-up shower.

Armed with coffee and the Phoenix Gazette, I settled into my easy chair. At that moment, life was good, and I didn't have a care in the world until the phone rang.

"Hello?" I answer guardedly.

"Morning, Jack, and Merry Christmas. This is Sergeant Dobbs. Because of the holiday, I'm working the switchboard today."

"What's up, Sarge?" I ask, waiting for the *awe shit* news.

"Two things. Detective Kowalski left you a message to call him in his room when you can. The room number is ... " he rambled off the number along with his concern for Kowalski.

I interrupted his speech about Stan's popularity, which almost resembled a eulogy. It wasn't one, but it felt a bit maudlin.

I interrupt, "What about number two?"

"Oh, yeah, that," he says apologetically. "One of our night patrols found a gunshot victim slumped over the steering wheel of a stolen Trans AM."

I ask, "A black Trans?"

"Yeah, how'd you know?"

"Lucky guess," I say. "And who was the onsite investigator?"

"Grayson Donelly."

This was a huge break in the case. Although I had differences with Donelly, he wasn't a backstabber and wouldn't try to steal my thunder. Of course, it was too early to confirm the ballistics report and the victim's ID. I took a sip of my tepid coffee and realized my idyllic Christmas Day had ended.

* * *

When I strolled into headquarters and approached the duty desk, a crowd of holiday revelers filled the room with predictable Christmas offenses. Most of them probably involved the use of alcohol or, better said, overuse.

Seeing me, the duty officer mockingly says, "Merry Christmas," stretching out his arms theatrically as if to envelop the throng inside.

"Yep," I say and ask, "I got a call from Dobbs, who told me about a homicide. You know where the report is?"

"Yeah, it's still on Donelly's desk," he says and motions toward the back.

Using my key, I unlock the office door. I reach for the light switch and flip on the overhead fluorescent tubes. My presence was one of those rare moments when the department was void of people. At the rear of the office, Donelly's desk, covered in folders, looked bureaucratic. Awards populated the wall, and meticulously arranged folders with labeling that could never be mistaken for anything other than their indicated markings.

"I'll give you A plus for organization," I say out loud to the empty room.

As promised, the folder labeled December 24 earned its importance dead center on the desk. After picking it up, I retreated to my hovel, where my lack of organizational skills was on full display. In my defense, it's not that I don't show them, it's that I know where they are hidden— and as far as I'm concerned, that's all that matters.

As I open the folder, my attention was immediately drawn to the Polaroid photo paper clipped to the inside pocket. It was an unflattering profile image of Paul Grendon slumped over the steering column with a repulsive hole in his right temple. I recognized him from his prison photo that Emily Ruger handed me the day before. I was confident when Ballistics issued their report that the bullet would match the ones responsible for the death of Jackson. And as far as looking for the black Trans AM, we have it, leaving the search for it now pointless. This was a planned hit. The pieces were falling into place. The killer, an attractive redhead—my guess, to gain a greater share of whatever they were looking for. She must have another accomplice, because you just don't off somebody in a remote area, then find a phone booth to call for a cab.

I began reviewing the list of items found on the body, but noticed that the car's contents were blank—not even an air freshener. Grendon was another story. There was a hotel receipt from Winslow dated only a couple of days ago and a receipt from the Mexicali Bistro. He had loose change, cigarettes, chewing gum, and a ballpoint pen. That was his total inventory. The pieces were falling into place.

"Mmm," I began thinking. *Winslow is about sixty miles away. If the traffic is light, I should be able to make it in less than an hour and still get back in time for my dinner date with Jessica. I gotta follow this lead.*

Chapter Thirty-Five

Sometimes you win, and sometimes you lose, I thought as I battled sleepiness. My eyes strained forward, and my back let me know I had pushed myself too hard. The ride to Winslow proved helpful, but it added another layer of mystery. All the people I talked with said yeah, they remembered the man, but were vague about the woman with him. Cassie, the waitress, was the only one who remembered anything significant. She recalled the woman's ring when she paid the bill. According to her, what she remembered most was that she paid for the meal in cash and then left a big tip. According to her, she appeared to be in charge, in her words, "A boss of a corporation." When I showed her the Polaroid photo, she got squeamish, but confirmed it was the man who was with her. She added something noteworthy. She told me that when the couple left the restaurant, a guy sitting alone left at the same time, appearing to following them. Unfortunately, her recollection of him was that he was a tall German and a lousy tipper.

Okay, first, Jackson is removed from sharing the prize, whatever it is. Then Paul Grendon is eliminated. Is the mysterious woman the last man standing, or does she have a new partner? And who is he?

I glance at my watch—*five-ten. I could possibly make it to the hotel by a little past six.* I push down hard on the accelerator.

* * *

The parking situation was bumper-to-bumper around the hotel. For the sake of expediency, I turned on my hazard lights and double-parked. Fortunately, the lobby was empty, and most of the activity came from the adjoining bar. When I turned the corner, the girl at the counter was the same one I had talked to the last time I was there.

Approaching, she beams and says, "Merry Christmas, Detective."

"And Merry Christmas to you, too."

I didn't want to go into too many niceties, so I ask, "I was supposed to meet one of your guests for dinner at six. Do you suppose you could ring her room it's—"

"I'm afraid you just missed them, Detective." Her eyes travel to the wall clock, and says, "It's 6:30. Miss Jaeger was here in the lobby a short time ago. After around 6:20 or so, she left with friends. By their conversation, I assume they are going to dinner."

I ask, "Did they mention where?"

"No, sir," she says and forces a smile.

"Okay, thanks." I head for the door.

Once outside, I took a deep breath and considered my alternatives. Not having the slightest idea where they would go for dinner, I thought it would be better to call it a night. Still wanting to see Jessica before she leaves, the only option was the early morning meeting at the train station.

Chapter Thirty-Six

As my alarm sounded, I thought, *it can't be the time to get up; I just went to bed.* Once my eyes adjusted, the digital display said it was 4:01 a.m. I fought the urge to roll over and go back to sleep, but knew I would miss the last chance to see Jessica. I flipped off my covers and planted my bare feet on the cold floor. That in itself woke me. I headed for the bathroom.

Shortening my morning routine to save time, I splashed water on my face and did a quick brushing of my teeth and a spritz of cologne. I assumed the latter would be necessary when I got close enough to Jessica for it to matter. I skipped shaving because I intended to return to bed for a while before officially starting my day. Kowalski, the mother hen, would not be timing my arrival. So I thought, *what the hell, I'll get there when I get there.*

The morning chill slapped me in the face as I stepped outside, and the falling snowflakes completed the job of waking me. The light accumulation of snow on my car showed it had only recently begun, and a couple of swipes of blades cleared them from my windshield.

Not surprisingly, the day after Christmas, the traffic was light, so I arrived in plenty of time before Jessica's train departure. Approaching the station on San Francisco Street, I made a left into the parking lot.

After exiting my car, I took the lower walkway that ran parallel to the old Route 66 and entered the ticket office.

Babs was the first one to spot me and yell, "Here comes the sheriff," as if she were in a cheap Saturday matinee western. All eyes of the dozen or so people who clustered together in the terminal fell on me. I had a compelling urge to draw my weapon and use it on her.

She held out her wrists, signaling me to cuff her. "Take me in, officer, for I've been a bad girl."

A collective snicker moved throughout the room.

"Babs, shut up!" implored Jessica as she came in between the two of us. "You're embarrassing us." She points to a corner of the room. "Go, sit down over there."

Babs gave Jessica a sloppy salute and staggered off.

I felt the uncomfortable sting of the curious.

No doubt sensing my unease, Jessica says, "I know it's cold, but I think we would be more comfortable outside."

I nod and turn to leave, pushing our way out. We move away from the entrance but remain close to the building.

Jessica asks, "What happened to you last night? I stayed in the lobby for a while, but Babs and her *new love* got impatient."

I said, "It turned out I missed you by about five minutes."

"Jack, I wish I had known that. I even checked with the desk to see if you left me a message."

I apologize. "I'm sorry about that. I was so eager to get here on time that I didn't want to waste time and stop for a call. Did you have a good time?"

She laughs. "Good time? Ha! I tell you if I wasn't that hungry, I would have preferred to stay in my room. You just saw how obnoxious Babs can be. Well, I was the third wheel in a very uncomfortable trio."

I couldn't help but smile. "Honestly, Jessica, I don't know how you even have her as a friend."

"When she's sober, she's a lot of fun," says Jessica. "And honestly, I need all the laughter I can get right now. But enough about her. I'm just happy you are here to say goodbye."

Honestly, I was asking myself why I was here. Maybe it was out of pity or just plain remorse for everything that transpired between us. There was this awful pause, and I didn't know what to say. Yeah, me, the guy with all the smart-ass remarks is now silent.

Breaking the silence, she asks, "Jack?"

"Yeah?"

"I-I was just realizing we aren't J&J anymore."

Jessica looks straight into my eyes and bawls. I bring her into my arms and caress her back. She looks up at me through a veil of tears and says, "I know."

After a few minutes of silence, she draws back, wipes the tears away from her face, and forces a smile. "Jack, I better get back in there before Babs starts to make out with some wife's husband."

We both laugh.

More composed now, she asks, "If I write to you, will you write back?"

I say, "Of course," and kiss her on the cheek.

She goes for the door, and I hold it open. I began to follow, but she raises a hand. "Jack, we better say our goodbyes here—it's painful enough."

I nod. She unexpectedly clings to me and gives me a long kiss before abruptly turning away. I stop momentarily in the open doorway and watch her blend into the collection of waiting passengers. I let the door close, never looking back to see if she turned to see me one last time.

Chapter Thirty-Seven

Doug lay on his couch, staring at the ceiling. It was a couple of days past Christmas; he had worked his night shift and was beat. Someone had gotten sick in the elevator, an ice machine went on the fritz, and worst of all, he had to call the police because of rowdiness between families. *Yeah, Merry Christmas, he thought.* The knock on the door startled him. His hand searched under the seat cushion for his revolver. He twisted off the couch, held the gun behind his back, and cracked open the blinds. It was Ralph.

He returned his gun to its hiding place and went to the door.

"Hey, man whazzhapping?" shouts Ralph, glassy-eyed and obviously under the influence of something.

"Nothing," says Doug dolefully, stepping back to allow Ralph to enter. "What's up with you?"

"I still have to pick up the trash, man. You'd be surprised how much shit people deep-six after Christmas," says Ralph, taking off his heavy jacket.

"I thought we'd wait maybe, you know, like in spring," says Doug, slowly drifting back to the couch.

"You're harshing my mellow!" exclaims Ralph. "Cody's on my case. Now that he's got the gold scent, he wants the action."

Doug plops onto the cushion. "Ralph, the cops are sniffing around, and I don't like it."

"Hey, man, it's not like you committed the murder of that guy," says Ralph.

"It's Jackson. The guy's name was Jackson, and I feel kind of sorry for him. I'm just afraid the cops will be on me like white on rice for withholding evidence. I just don't think we should do anything right now," says Doug.

Ralph brings one of the kitchen chairs and places the flip side toward Doug. Straddling the seat like a cowboy, he rests both of his arms on its back. "Doug, you know we need Cody. Now that we cut him into the deal, he's psyched and ready to go."

"Why can't he wait until spring?" asks Doug.

"You don't get it, man," insists Ralph. "That's when he makes his bread."

Doug nods. "Okay, tell Cody that we'll start the first week after New Year's Day. You think he'll be alright with that?"

"Totally, man," says Ralph. "Now, let's pardy, hardy."

Chapter Thirty-Eight

Although it was several days past Christmas when he entered the squad room, the trimmings of the season still graced its interior. It was strange not to see Kowalski sitting at his desk with his irritated expression, showing his annoyance with a quick glance at the clock on the wall. My visit with him yesterday boosted my morale, knowing he was on the mend and, after some rehab, would be joining me. With or without him, I still had two murders on my plate.

Sitting down, I caught a glimpse of Emily Ruger coming out of the back room and moving toward me. She stopped in front of my desk and says, "Good morning, and a belated Merry Christmas. How did you spend the day?"

Her greeting wasn't what I would call sincere, but more sarcastic. "I did fine spending my time having a scotch or two with Santa's elves."

She didn't look amused. Instead, she says, "I may be helping you in Kowalski's absence, but don't you think that I should be working from his desk, up front here, rather than in the back room?"

After my not-so-pleasant holiday respite, I didn't need her whining. "Who said you had to stay in the back?"

"Well, ... ah, no one," she mutters. "I-I just thought—"

"Listen," *I was tempted to say, doll, but thought better of it, sparing myself a trip to HR.* "Let's not make this a big deal. Kowalski won't be back for some time, so you bring your stuff over and settle in. If you haven't already, you will notice that he is a neat freak." I aim my thumb behind me toward Kowalski's desk. "So, just try not to mess up his stuff. Okay?"

She nods, forces a smile, and says, "Okay." She turns away.

I say, "Hold on a sec. Once you move in, we need to discuss the case."

Without saying a word, she resumes her exit while I pin the new information to the case board on the wall next to my desk.

I was just about finished when Ruger returned with her purse, a large folder that looked like an expandable file, and a briefcase. Setting her stuff on Kowalski's desk, she turns to me and says, "Okay, boss, reporting for service."

Spare me the sarcasm. I bit my tongue. "By the way, how was your holiday?" I ask, trying to get our relationship back on a smooth track.

She rolls her desk chair over to my side. "Nothing much. I don't have relatives here, and I'm still trying to get acquainted with the town. I went to Christmas Mass, which was about the extent of my social life."

"Well, to tell you the truth, those pesky elves weren't much company. And other than a trip to Winslow, my holiday festivities didn't amount to too much either."

She laughs. Finding her laughter contagious, I join in. This was the first time I saw her let go. I found it refreshing to see another side of her personality.

I lean back on my chair, rest my elbows on my armrests, and cup my hands together. "You know a lot about this case already, but over the holiday, Paul Grendon turns up dead."

She points toward his picture on the wall. "Yeah, that's the mug shot I got from the Northern Nevada Correctional Center."

"Well, we got this dame ... " I pause and look at Ruger.

She smiles, "Call her anything you want, just don't ever call me that."

I continue, "So far, we haven't been able to determine her true identity. Perhaps we'll get some usable prints when we have the crime lab report."

Ruger says, "When I got Grendon's picture, I requested the visitor log for both Jackson, a.k.a. Oscar Burrows, and his cellmate, Paul Grendon."

I nod approvingly. "Good. When I mentioned my trip to Winslow, that was business. I found a restaurant's check in Grendon's pocket. Thinking the waitress might remember something of importance, I took a ride to interview her. As it turns out, the only thing I could glean from the visit was our mysterious woman may have been *the* operation's ringleader, and perhaps there's another character in her gang."

"Okay, what's our next move?" asks Ruger.

I point toward the picture of the Weatherford. "I think the answer is here."

Chapter Thirty-Nine

I called the Weatherford Hotel earlier to ensure the owner, Henry Taylor, would be there. As Emily Rugar and I turned the corner to the hotel's front desk, an attractive blonde woman stood on the opposite side of the desk, conversing with Jean, the assistant manager. She turned and greeted us with one of those smiles that stay with you forever.

Before I could offer a reply, she extends a hand. "You must be Detective Owens. I'm Pamela Green, but everyone calls me Sam. My husband, Henry, and I are co-owners."

I take her hand. "Yes, I called earlier to meet with him. My partner, Detective Ruger," I motion toward her, "and I have a few questions that he may have the answers to a case we are working on."

She asks, "Is it that murder several weeks ago in the Double-Six Hotel?"

I nod. Hoping to avoid discussing it, I quickly interject, "Yes, but I'm not free to say much about it."

"No, I understand," she replies. "It's just one of those things that isn't good for business. And speaking about business, you must be about yours, and I must be about mine. Please follow me, Detectives."

She leads us back to the lobby and then abruptly turns to the right, down a set of stairs. My first impression of the basement was its low ceiling and the collection of tools, sawhorses, and a collage of wire, pipe, and lumber scattered on the floor. About mid-point stood Henry, hunched over a makeshift workbench, involved in restorative work on a light fixture.

Seeing us, he says, "Welcome to the mess."

He was tall, bearded, with slightly graying hair protruding from the sides of a baseball cap. He was at least a head taller than his wife, but if smiles indicated compatibility, they were a perfect match.

The three of us walked to the work area and, in doing so, had to duck under a support beam, where we joined Henry. He reached out and shook our hands. Gesturing with an open hand, he says, "Someday, this will be the resurrection site of The Gopher Hole. Right now, it's my workshop and storage area for more pressing projects. So, what do you need from us, Detective?"

"Jean, your assistant manager, told me your hotel originally had forty-two rooms."

Both Henry and Sam nodded.

"I'm interested in room 209. I understand you have the architectural drawings. Can you show me where it's located in those drawings?"

"That's an easy request," says Henry, pointing upward. "I have those in my office upstairs. Please follow me."

Using the same course as our previous descent, we move upward as the stairs creak underfoot. We retrace our steps to the front lobby and then make a sharp turn up another set of stairs. Following him, we enter the office, which has a low ceiling and windows set only one foot above the vintage, open-gaped flooring. A couple of four-drawer metal file cabinets dominate the center of the room, surrounded by desks and their overcrowded tops. The stacks of memorabilia spilling out of cardboard boxes gave me the feeling that I was in a museum archivist's workshop. Complimenting this collage of an industrious workplace, a singular potted plant added a bit of sparkle to an otherwise cheerless room.

"Let's see," Henry mutters, approaching a frame on the back wall and squinting. "This is it," he announces firmly, tapping his index finger on the glass. "The architect never identified the rooms with actual room numbers. See, it's only labeled 'room #9.'"

Moving closer to the drawing, I ask, "Is it possible to have a look at that room?"

"That may be a bit of a problem. The old 209 is now part of room 203. You see, in the 1900s, you were lucky enough to get a bed and nightstand. And if you think you'll find something under the floorboards, they were ripped up during the remodel—although I did find something."

"And what was that?" I ask.

"Some wine bottles and a few Anheuser-Busch beer bottles. I can show them to you if you would like."

"No, thank you, but I still would like to have a look at the room."

With some reluctance, Henry says, "Okay, follow me."

Henry knocked on the door of room 203, saying, "Even though the room's listed as unoccupied, I always think it best not to surprise anyone —including myself." He laughs.

The door opens to a spacious room, no doubt combining several original rooms. The queen-sized gondola sleigh bed featured two matching side cabinets, each topped with an ornate table lamp. A couple of wing-backed, sitting chairs were placed on either side of a gas-powered simulation fireplace. To complete the room, a couch sat at the end of the bed, facing the wall, where a television appeared out of place on a dresser.

I watch as Henry walks to the center of the room, just about even with the couch, and says, "This is where room 209 used to be."

Chapter Forty

Feeling frustrated by the apparent dead end at the Weatherford Hotel, I suggested that Ruger dig a little further into the prison's visitors' log. At the same time, I pay Kowalski a visit at the hospital. Her eagerness almost made me feel she was only too happy for us to part company. If that were indeed the case, I'd give her a few more weeks for my charming personality to grow on her.

Hospitals are not one of my favorite places, but the hot nurses make up for the smell of antiseptic and the annoying beeping of monitors. Although I had visited him earlier since he was hospitalized to check on his condition, this visit was more of a pick-your-brain session.

As I enter Stan's room, he gives me one of his toothy smiles. It's a giveaway that he is happy to see me despite saying, "Hey, I came here to get better."

"Glad to see you, too, Stan," I say while reaching out to shake his hand. "I would have brought you some chocolates, but I ate them while driving here."

"It's just as well," he says. "Those days are over for a while. Sit down and tell me the real reason you're here."

"It shows that much, uh?"

I reposition the chair next to the bed and sit down. "You're the local history buff in this area. I probably could have gone to the library, but I figured you would save me a lot of trouble."

"I don't know if I'm that much of an expert, but what's your question?"

"Several weeks ago, you talked about that 1889 robbery east of Tucson. Seeing we are interested in treasure hunters, what do you know about buried treasure in this area?

Stan reaches over to his bedside table and takes a sip of water from his Styrofoam cup.

"There are many stories of stagecoach and train robberies in this state. They all seem to roll together. The one most fascinating occurred in 1881 near Canyon Diablo—"

"Stan, why didn't you tell me about that one instead of the one near Tucson?"

I see Stan turn red.

"I guess that was the first one that came to mind because the robbers were captured and, after a sensational trial, weren't found guilty.

"Okay. So, what about the Canyon Diablo robbery?"

"That robbery, too, involved a stagecoach. It carried $100,000 in cash, $2,500 in silver dollars, and $40,000 in gold coins—that's the 1881 value."

I ask, "How do you know so much about that one?"

Stan sheepishly grins. "My boys and I went on our own treasure hunt a couple of years after arriving here."

I laugh. "Somehow, Stan, I don't see you as some kinda treasure hunter."

"I was younger, and it was one of those bonding things with my boys. Anyway, we went up to a place called Veit Springs. That's where the gang of five escaped after the holdup. It wasn't called that at the time, but just an unnamed area four or five miles west of the San Francisco Peak. It got its present name from George Veit. He, too, was interested in the treasure and bought up the land so he could dig for the stolen treasure."

I say, "From what you are telling me, he never found the loot, right?"

Stan takes another sip of water. "Yeah, but later, I thought it would have been pretty difficult to transport all that gold and silver while high-tailing it up that rough terrain."

I ask, "What happened to those guys? The robbers, I mean?"

"All killed in a shootout at their hideout."

"So, what I gather, you now think the gold and silver were buried somewhere along their escape route?"

Stan nods. "And I'm too old and my boys are more interested in girls than for us to be searching from Canyon Diablo to Veit Springs. That's about fifty miles of what-if. No, thank you."

Captivated by Stan's story, I lean back in my chair and let out a sigh of bewilderment. "So, you think the murders are linked to that one?"

"I do now, after considering everything. Of course, I may be wrong because of the number of actual stagecoach robberies in this state. I'll be glad when I can get out of this hospital and get back to my desk."

For a moment, I hesitate to break the news to Stan. Finally, I say, "You may find your desk a bit crowded."

"How, so?" Stan asks.

"Um, Emily Ruger's using it until you get back."

Stan's monitor spikes a bit.

"I hope you told her to keep it neat?"

"Nah, I told her to make herself at home and don't worry about making a mess—you like it that way."

The monitor spikes again.

"Are you trying to give me another heart attack?"

"No, it's only my sick sense of humor, Stan."

"Yeah, Jack, that's what I miss about you."

I get up and extend my hand. Stan takes it, and we shake. His grip isn't what it used to be, but he makes a strong effort. "I gotta go. I'll keep you up to date, and thanks for the history lesson."

"I think I'll be out of here in a few days. You're welcome to stop by the house and get the lecture from Mary."

I grin and wave goodbye.

Chapter Forty-One

Doug McGuire and Ralph Tyler huddle around an Arizona highway map centered on the table in Ralph's trailer.

Cody Dosela nudges his way in, plunks a topographic map of Flagstaff area over it, and smooths it out without saying a word. Doug eyes Ralph. Ralph only shrugs and resumes slurping Old Milwaukee beer from a can. Doug appears bewildered and then takes a sip from his coffee mug.

"You got that note?" asks Cody.

Doug reaches into his inside coat pocket and retrieves a small envelope containing the matchbook from the old KOA hotel and Detective Owens's business card. He removes the defunct hotel's card and lays it on the map. He sets the envelope aside.

Cody studies the numbers and, without hesitation, points. "We start here," says Cody, pointing at a spot south of Interstate 40 named Two Guns.

"How do you know that's the starting point?" asks Doug.

Tapping his finger at the top number, Cody says, "Says so here. Let's go."

Just as fast as Cody laid down the map, he refolds it along with the envelope and tucks it under his arm. He makes his way toward the door.

"It's cold out there, Ralph," says Doug. "How about filling my thermos with some coffee?"

"Sure thing, kemo sahbee."

Cody shoots Ralph a look of disapproval and says, "I'll wait in Bronco."

"Are we gonna ride with you?" asks Doug.

Cody, his massive hand already holding the doorknob, turns and says, "No, you follow me."

The door closes, and Ralph says, "Hey, man, I'm hungry. Shouldn't we stop at Mr. Bob's? first"

"I don't think your buddy Cody's gonna waste time eating. My guess he's already brought food for himself. And he doesn't impress me as the sort of guy who shares."

Ralph says, "All I got is some baloney and bread. I'll scratch together a couple of sandwiches."

"That works," says Doug.

Halfway through preparing their food, they hear a loud blast from Cody's Bronco's horn.

"Shit, that guy's impatient," says Doug.

"I told you, man," says Ralph. "The guy's a little strange. You go out there and try to cool his jets. I'll finish up."

"Okay, okay. You got any Coke in your fridge?"

"Yeah, man. Grab a couple of cans first. Tell him I'll be out like Flint."

Doug laughs, "You mean, 'in like Flint.'"

"Whatever. Just tell him to cut me some slack, okay, Bud?"

Doug nods. "Sure thing, pal, but he's your friend. Shouldn't you be talking to him?"

"He's not really my friend. He's more like a homeboy."

"Okay, I'll go," says Doug and heads for the door, but before reaching it, another blast from Cody's horn urges them on.

Chapter Forty-Two

With Cody Dosela in the lead, the duo convoy exits Highway 40 at mile marker 230. At the end of the off-ramp, they take a sharp right, pass the abandoned gas station silhouetted by the rising sun, and continue down the road. They stop short of the old KOA campground pool. Ralph swings out of the passenger side of the Pacer, walks a short distance, then relieves himself with an audible sigh. Doug, too, finds a suitable spot and does the same, but with less fanfare.

Doug and Ralph join Cody while he removes his equipment from the Bronco.

"Need any help?" asks Doug.

"Here, take this," he says, handing him a walkie-talkie.

"What's this for?" asks Doug.

"I want you to go there," Cody points towards the freeway.

"And do what?"

"You, Ralph, you take this." Cody pulls out a survey staff meter and gives it to Ralph.

Cody points again and says, "You go out by that frontage road near freeway, and I'll tell you how to move it."

Ralph says, "That's it?"

"Yeah, that's it. Now go," Cody commands.

At the AMC Pacer, Ralph points. "How we suppose' to get this big ruler into that midget car?"

"Get in the car and open up the window. I'll hand it to you, and you just have to hang onto it."

"Hey, amigo, it's freakin' cold. And I didn't bring any gloves."

"You'll live. It's only a short ride," says Doug. "Besides, think about the treasure. You'll be able to buy all the gloves you'll ever want."

"Okay, Bud, but make sure you turn up the car's sauna."

With the survey staff resting between the Pacer's side mirror and door frame, they make their way toward the freeway's frontage road. While passing the abandoned gas station, Ralph notices a maroon 1979 Oldsmobile Cutlass parked under the station's canopy. "Hey man, that car wasn't there when we first got here. Whoever sees us, ain't they gonna wonder what we're up to?"

"Nah," says Doug. "People stop here all the time, most just to take a nap."

"Well, I sure would be rubbernecking anyone who drives a minicar with a bodacious ruler sticking out of it."

Doug says, "Relax, pal. We're going to be far enough away for anyone to notice what we're up to."

Arriving near the place Cody pointed to, Doug gets out and moves to the passenger side of the car. He pulls out the staff, walks a few feet west along the paved road, and plants it. A small puff of dirt marks the spot.

While holding the walkie-talkie, Ralph joins Doug. With the swiftness of a person who is bursting with treasure fever, he mashes down the talk button and says, "We are here, man."

Cody's staticky voice replies, "Move about three yards west. Over."

As Doug follows the instructions, Ralph quips, "Hey, man, I can hardly see him at this distance."

"He's got some sort of telescope on that tripod," says Doug. "Ralph, go and get my binoculars from the glove compartment."

Ralph returns, sets down the walkie-talkie, and puts the binoculars to his eyes. He says, "It looks like he's writing something down on the hood of his Bronco."

Doug says, "Here, hold this stick and let me have a peek."

As Doug has his turn, Cody's voice breaks the frigid air. "Go south down gravel road. We meet at the ruins. Over."

Ralph says, "Gotcha, man ... ah, over."

Following the same routine of handling the survey staff, they make their way toward a dilapidated wall, its one-time purpose denoted as "Mountain Lions" drawn over a remaining archway.

As Doug comes to a stop, Ralph says, "Keep the engine going, man, so that I can get some heat."

While waiting for Cody, Ralph huddles partly under the dashboard, trying to soak up whatever warmth he can.

"I don't know why you're such a baby, Ralph. You don't get cold when you're out picking up trash?"

"No. My gig is to drive the truck. My crew, that's their bag."

They both focus on a line of dust trailing behind Cody's truck. A wash of dirt overcomes Cody's Bronco as it comes to an abrupt stop, momentarily enveloping the vehicle. Before the fog settles, Cody is out of his truck and heads toward Doug and Ralph.

Cody raises his arm and points again to the freeway, only several yards to the right. "Now you go back to that spot and hold the survey staff."

Doug asks, "Why didn't you tell us just to move when we were there already?"

Cody, appearing unfazed, says, "Go, I'll set up here."

Doug rolls his eyes and motions toward Ralph. "C'mon, pal."

In the Pacer, Doug says, "I'm getting to dislike that guy."

"Yeah, man, he's a real downer."

Following the same road, they came in on—they head out toward the interstate.

Tightly gripping the steering wheel, Doug grumbles, "Go, I'll set up here. He's acting as if he's the boss and we are his slaves. He forgets we are partners. Right, Ralph?"

"Hey, man, I'm just interested in the buried loot. Once we dig it up, we'll split company."

"Yeah, yeah, I know. It's just the crap we have to put up with."

They reach their destination, and Doug exits the car and approaches the passenger side.

Again, Doug takes the surveyor's staff and positions himself where he thinks Cody pointed.

While Doug held the staff, Ralph used the binoculars to check on Cody. "He's not aiming that gizmo at us. Doug, don't you think that's wacko?"

"Everything about this situation is wacko. What's he doing now?"

Ralph holds up the binoculars. "He's writing on the map again. I guess that's cool, right?"

Doug nods and says, "I suppose. After all, he's the surveyor."

"Hold on, pal," Ralph says. "He's got two maps, one on top of the other. You think he's stiffing us?"

"Dunno. Maybe, but the other one might be the roadmap."

Ralph says, "Now, I'm starting to get bummed."

The walkie-talkie comes alive. "Okay. Meet me at Canyon Diablo Bridge. Over."

Doug looks at Ralph and says, "Maybe we are being a little paranoid?'

"No sweat. We've come this far to turn back."

Packing the equipment into the Pacer again, they start for the bridge.

Doug says, "I'm gonna go past the Lion place again. I wanna stay on that gravel road. It seems like the better option."

"We're gonna hook up with the old Route 66 road," says Ralph.

"What's left of it," says Doug. "And I don't plan on driving this car on that bridge, either."

"Hey man, you flying?" asks Ralph.

"Why, there's no speed limit here?"

"Don't freak out, man, but we got company."

"Huh?"

"Looks like Smokey's taken an interest in us."

Chapter Forty-Three

When I got back to the station, I found Emily Ruger sitting at her desk, or I should say, at Kowalski's desk. She had this look of, *I know something you don't know.*

She asks, "Well, how's Stan doing?"

I slide into my chair and swivel around to face her. "He's doing fine. He's looking forward to reclaiming his desk." I ask, "What have you been up to?"

She smiles. "While you two boys have been chewing the fat and reminiscing about the good ol' days, I've been burning up the wires talking to the Northern Nevada Correctional Center staff. At first, I was more interested in the visitor log of Jackson, aka Oscar Burrows. He really didn't have any steady visitors, except his ex-wife, for a while. She later divorced him."

"Okay. So, what about Paul Grendon?"

"Remember, I said they were cell-mates?"

I nod.

"They shared a cell for only a year. That's when I found out about Paul Grendon's visitor."

I hold up my hand. 'I'm a bit confused."

"Yep, so was I," she says. "Both men served in the Northern Nevada

Correctional Center but were not cellmates then. When the prison system opened a new facility called Stewart Conservation Camp in 1978, that's when they began sharing living quarters."

I ask, "So, I'm guessin' that is when they hatched their plan?"

She says, "That's what I think. But here's the most interesting part. Grendon had a female visitor called Valerie Vaughn, but only maybe once a month when he was in the Northern Correctional Center."

I ask, "But after he was transferred?"

"Almost every week," says Ruger.

"I think I know what happened."

"The plan to go after buried treasure was hatched in the Stewart Conservation Camp, right?" Ruger asks rhetorically.

"That makes sense," I agree. "But the fourth person, where does he fit in?"

"I wondered that, too," she says. "This is my theory: Valerie was seeing someone else while Grendon was doing time. Burrows, aka Jackson, tells Grendon of the treasure, and he tells his girlfriend Valerie. She, in turn, tells her boyfriend, and the double cross is worked out."

"That's my theory, too."

Ruger nods. "Yep, great minds think alike. Did Kowalski have anything to say about the case, or was your visit strictly, like I said, *reminiscing 'bout the good ol' days*?"

"Oh, how you women misjudge us men."

Ruger laughs. "I'm right ... right?"

I reply, "Maybe a little, but I think I know what treasure they are after. It was a gold and silver heist from a stagecoach in 1881 near Canyon Diablo."

"So, we're gonna solve a crime from the Old West days?"

"Yep. Now, all we need is a picture of Valerie Vaughn."

Ruger says, "It's in the works. I expect to get a faxed picture of her from the Nevada DMV any minute now."

"And a glossy?"

"Any day, now," says Ruger.

I reply with exuberance, "Well then, giddy-up!"

Chapter Forty-Four

The Arizona Highway Patrol Ford Grand Victoria pulls behind Doug's Pacer and briefly turns on its double-dome flashing lights. Both vehicles slow to a halt.

"Shit, what are goin' to tell the cop?" asks Doug. "I've been here several times, and no one has ever questioned me."

Ralph laughs. "Yeah, man, but this is the first time you gotta big ruler poking outa your car."

Doug shuts off the engine and glances over his shoulder. "He's not coming out."

"He's running your plates, man. That's what they do on the boob tube. Five-O's making sure you ain't some criminal."

"I don't know, Ralph, I'm starting to get worried about this."

"Cool it, man. Here he comes. Roll down your window."

The officer, his hand at the ready on his holstered pistol, ducks down to look into the interior. "What are you boys up to?"

Doug begins, "We're going ... to ... ah ... um—"

"We're looking for buried treasure," says Ralph.

The officer smiles broadly, then laughs. "Yeah, I sorta thought so, with that device you got sticking out of your car. I see you are heading toward the Diablo Bridge. When you're out trying to find your treasure, be careful around those canyon walls. There are a lot of loose rocks around there. I don't want to have to come back here to pick up your bodies."

Doug says, "We'll be careful, officer."

"And one more thing. The sun's gonna set around five-thirty. Even with the moon nearly full, I wouldn't chance riding around this area in the dark."

"Yes, sir. We understand," says Doug.

The patrolman goes back to his cruiser.

Doug and Ralph exhale in relief.

Doug turns on the ignition and then resumes heading toward the bridge.

When they arrive, they park next to Cody's Bronco. They see Cody is in the middle, his tripod already set up.

They leave the car and walk toward him, the loose gravel crunching loudly beneath their feet.

"What cop want?" asks Cody when they approach.

Doug says, "Just wanted to know what we were up to."

"What you tell 'im?"

"We said we were looking for treasure," says Ralph.

Uncharacteristically, Cody laughs.

Ralph trades glances with Doug.

Doug says, "Hey, man, my stomach's barking—when we gonna eat?"

Cody points in a southwesterly direction. "See tower?"

"Yeah," says Doug.

"That's Cundiff's Tower Station."

"I know. I've been here many times."

"You go eat there while I'll still work."

"Then what?"

"I take one more measurement, then done."

"When you're finished, will you know where the treasure is?" Doug asks.

"Maybe. Now go, the sun is getting lower."

"C'mon, Ralph. Let's get going."

Back at the car, Ralph once again slides into the passenger side while Doug guides the survey staff through the open window.

Doug gets into the driver's seat, starts the engine, and eases the AMC Pacer past Cody. Not looking at them as they pass, he appears absorbed in aiming his transit at the highway.

Ralph asks, "What's he looking at?"

"Dunno. Maybe he's seeing something we can't see through that scope of his?"

Reaching the stone tower, Doug helps Ralph with the surveyor's pole and leans it against the car. "No sense in taking this with us. Let's go up those steps and get out of this wind. Ralph, grab the bi-nocks. I want to keep an eye on Cody."

"You got it, pal."

Doug goes up a couple of steps and leans back against the tower's curved wall. He opens the paper bag, pulls out the sandwiches, and hands one to Ralph. Once more, he reaches into the bag for the Coke, keeping one for himself before handing one down to Ralph.

"What are you going to do with your share of the treasure, Ralph?"

Ralph appears to mull over the question as he begins to eat. "Man, I'm going to split and hang out on the beach in Santa Monica. Maybe get discovered and get into the movies."

Doug laughs. "Like what kinda roles?"

"Don't be a downer. Hey, talent like mine is in demand. Maybe I'll play the heavy in *The Rockford Files.*"

"Before you get ahead of yourself, maybe we need to find the gold first?"

"A man can dream, can't he?" says Ralph before taking another bite of his sandwich.

Doug gets up, takes a quick look with his binoculars at Cody, then sits back down.

"Still there?"

"Yeah. He's doing something with that map."

The walkie-talkie comes to life. "Doug?"

Doug shoves the last bit of his sandwich into his mouth, picks up the walkie-talkie, and mumbles, "Uhuh."

"Hold the stick at the base of the tower. Over."

Doug runs to the car, retrieves the survey staff, and rushes back to the tower. Holding the rod in one hand and his mobile phone in the other, he says, "Ready ... ah, over."

After a couple of minutes, Cody finally says, "Done. Come back."

Once they return to the bridge, Cody discreetly collects his equipment.

"Hey, Cody," says Ralph. "What's up? Do you know where the treasure is?"

After depositing the staff in the back of the Bronco, Cody says, "I'll show you."

Grabbing the map off the Bronco's tailgate, Cody walks to the front of the vehicle. He spreads out the map on the hood and points broadly. "This area, near the old Route 66, is where the treasure is buried."

"Ah, that's a pretty big chunk of real estate," says Ralph. "You can't narrow it down?"

"Not sure of where start of angles. See, not sure where to start at pool, or lion place, or bridge. See, this side of the bridge or middle of bridge or this end of bridge ... all make a big difference with angle."

Doug asks, "So, what do we do now?"

"We come back another day—with a metal detector."

Chapter Forty-Five

My day started, as usual, with a cup of coffee and a lemon Danish roll. Unlike Kowalski's passion for the same morning treat, Ruger's obsession was more in line with granola and whatever normal people found unappealing. This craving of hers was easy on my pocketbook, which was a positive, but it hampered the conventional morning sit-down. So, in the cocoon of my self-indulgence of sugar and caffeine, I mull over the incident log. Each one was almost predictable: harassment complaint, disorderly intoxication, disorderly conduct, vehicle fire, and an injury accident on Interstate 40 east of Flagstaff. But what stood out in the mire of human misdeeds was an apparent murder at Two Guns. This is not to say murder doesn't happen in Arizona—it just takes on a different perspective when it is closer to home.

While thinking about the inhumanity of mankind, Ruger comes out of the break room, her cup in hand with a tea bag flopped over its side. "Morning, Jack," she says, not stopping until she reaches Kowalski's desk. She deposits her drink. "What's happening today?" Her question was more like a kid asking a parent when they are going to the beach.

"Good morning. For one, we should start distributing the faxed picture of Valerie Vaughn. It will at least be a start until we get the glossy from the Nevada DMV. Also, we should go to the Mexicali Bistro in Winslow with the picture, and also see if we can't get a better description of the other guy."

My phone rings, so I swivel my chair back to my desk.

"Detective Owens, speaking."

"This is Superintendent Bill Clark from the Arizona Department of Public Safety."

"So, what's up?" I ask.

"The only reason I'm calling you is that one of your department's business cards was found on the body of the deceased. Do you know a Cody Dosela?"

"Sorry, never heard the name."

"He's an Apache who lives off the res and works as a surveyor."

"Still no connection," I say, still wondering how he got my card.

"Maybe this will jog your memory," says Clark. "One of our highway patrolmen questioned a couple of guys who said they were looking for buried treasure. At that time, he didn't question the deceased, but now assumes they were working together."

"You got a name?" I ask.

"Yeah, he ran the plates. It was a yellow 1975 AMC Pacer belonging to Douglas J. McGuire. You know him?"

The name hit me like the proverbial ton of bricks. "I sure do. I questioned him a while back regarding the death of Samuel Jackson, also known as Oscar Burrows. He was murdered at the Double Six Hotel in December."

"I assume you'll want to see the body and check what we have as far as evidence?"

"I do."

"He's still at the Coconino Medical Examiner's office in Flagstaff. We are trying to locate family members."

"Bill, thanks for the call. We'll be there within the hour."

"What was that all about?" asks Ruger.

"A break in the Jackson case. That was Bill Clark from the Arizona Public Safety Department. A patrolman from their Highway Patrol Division found the body of Cody Dosela at the Twin Guns site."

Ruger says, "I never heard that name associated with the case?"

"Somehow, the deceased knows Doug McGuire. At this point, I don't know how."

"Now what?" asks Ruger.

I pick up the case file from my desk and wave it towards Ruger. "I'll get an arrest warrant from a judge. I want a couple of uniform officers with us to take him in for booking." I glance at my watch. "He works the night shift, so he's getting off work about now. He should be at his place by the time we get the warrant."

Chapter Forty-Six

As Ruger and I climb the stairs to Doug McGuire's apartment, I couldn't help but think about Kowalski's heart attack. Besides that incident, I fume inside over McGuire's apparent duplicity, concealing important facts about the Jackson case. At the top, Ruger and I position ourselves on either side of McGuire's doorway, while the two uniformed police officers moved to the side and behind me. From inside, there were the telltale clatters of a television broadcast. Cupping my hand into a fist, I used it like a hammer and slammed the metal door. "McGuire, police department, open the door!"

There was a scurry of activity inside before I heard the deadbolt slide open. McGuire opens the door, appearing bewildered. He took a couple of steps back. "What do you want? I didn't do anything wrong."

I pushed past the door, causing McGuire to retreat further.

Holding the warrant before me, I shake it in his direction. "Doug McGuire, I am arresting you on suspicion of the murder of Cody Dosela."

"Cody? Dead?" he utters, his face contorted in confusion. "I didn't kill him. The last time I saw him, he was still alive. What's this all about?"

Ruger says, "I suggest you remain silent." She reads him his Miranda Rights while one of the uniformed officers takes McGuire's hands and places handcuffs on him.

I put on my latex gloves and focus on the kitchen area, opening wall cabinets to check their interiors. I spot a shoebox that appeared out of place among the usual assortment of cooking utensils, plates, and pans. I pull it down to the top of the base and pop off the lid. Inside, I find a revolver wrapped in a cloth.

With the revolver visible and nesting in the cloth, I approach McGuire. "What's this?"

"It's my revolver. Once in a while, I go with my pal Ralph to go down to the desert and target practice."

"Was that the guy you were with at Two Guns?"

"Yeah, but we didn't kill anyone. We were with Cody, looking for buried treasure. We left first because Cody said he wanted to double-check his figures."

I take a whiff of the gun. "When was the last time you used this weapon?"

Doug stammers, "I-I-I don't remember. Maybe months ago. I didn't kill anyone."

"Okay, we'll continue this back at the station. Officer, book him and put him in a cell. Also, I want you to locate McGuire's pal Ralph."

Facing McGuire, I say, "Helping us will go a long way in your defense. I want you to give the office the name and address of your friend."

Looking pale and nervous, he says, "Ralph Tyler—he works for the Flagstaff's trash department. It's early. He's probably working."

I take an officer aside. "I'm going to call in a forensics team. Wait until they get here and then take McGuire to the station."

"What about Ralph Tyler?"

"After you check McGuire in, find Tyler and put him in a holding cell as a possible accomplice to the murder of Cody Dosela. Make sure he doesn't come in contact with McGuire."

"Will, do," says the officer, taking McGuire by the arm and leading him outside.

"And us?" asks Ruger.

"After the forensics team gets here, we're going to take a trip to Winslow and pay a visit to the Mexicali Bistro. This time, we have a picture of our mysterious lady, who, I'm sure, is bound to jog some memories."

Chapter Forty-Seven

Ruger wasn't much of a talker. I thought that maybe by getting away from the station, she might feel a bit more relaxed. It was just the opposite. We talked a little about the case, but when I asked her about her time in Phoenix, she clammed up tighter than my grandma's girdle.

By the time we arrive at the Mexicali Bistro, most of the lunch crowd had dissipated. Those remaining had apparently nothing else to do or only wanted a warm place to hang out. I spot Cassie, and she gave me the hiya nod.

The hostess greets us with a smile and says, "Good afternoon, folks. Table for two?"

"Yes, but we would like Cassie to wait on us."

She gives me an uncertain look and says, "Yes, sir, right this way."

We are led to a table at the back of the dining room. She hands us two menus. "Cassie will be with you in a minute."

I place my case folder to the side, then pick up my menu and tell Ruger, "I don't know about you, but I'm famished. I don't see any granola and grits. Maybe you have to ask for a special menu?"

Not amused by what I like to call my *down-home humor*, she says, "Maybe they can rustle me up a salad, partner?"

My smile was my only retort.

Cassie approaches our table, her order pad in hand. Before she could say anything, I opened my folder and pulled out the picture of Valerie Vaughn. "Is this the same woman that you saw with that man in the photograph I showed you the last time I was here?"

"Yep, that's her all right, but maybe a bit older than her picture."

"And you said that she was followed by a tall man?"

"Yep, I can now give you a better description of him."

I say, "That's funny. Usually, people's memories fade after a while."

"Oh, mine is fresh. He was with that woman as recently as yesterday. They came in for lunch, and he paid for the both of them. He still was a lousy tipper."

"And you didn't think of calling me?"

"Oh, I did, but I forgot your name and wasn't sure what police department you were with. You never gave me a card. So, I didn't think it was too important."

I was tempted to read her the riot act, but remained calm. Also, I was angry with myself for the omission. "How many times were they here before yesterday?"

"Just yesterday. They seemed to have an affection for each other—you know, their body language."

"Can you now give me a better description of the guy?"

"Sure. Like I said, he was tall, had a roundish face, almost baby-like, and sported a thick mustache. Oh, and another thing about the mustache—I think he wears it to hide his hairlip."

"His hair color?"

"Dark brown with some streaks of gray around his temple."

"And you didn't notice all that when I first saw you?"

"Hey, it was busy."

The hostess who greeted us earlier came over to our table. "Cassie, is everything okay?"

I speak up. "Yes, everything is fine. My girlfriend only wanted to know more about the salad selections."

Again, she gave me one of those questioning looks and walks away. Ruger, on the other hand, looked more interested in murder.

"Cassie, I'd like you to stop at the Flagstaff Police Station tomorrow, say, about ten?"

"No problem. I'm off on Thursdays. I usually go to Flagstaff to do my weekly grocery shopping. Now, are you going to order something?"

"Yeah, of course. I'll have the Reuben."

"And for you, Miss?"

"A large garden salad with a blue cheese dressing,"

Cassie turns, then halts. Turning back, she says, "I almost forgot."

To me, she appeared embarrassed.

"When that woman came here last time, she was with another fellow. Curious, I couldn't help myself and looked outside to see if they might be riding in the same car."

I smile, knowing she is thinking more along the lines of a cheating husband. "Yes, go on."

She blushed. "They went in the same car."

"Do you remember the make and model?"

"I do. It was a new Oldsmobile Cutlass. I know that for sure because my son's friend has one."

I ask, "The color?"

"Maroon."

Chapter Forty-Eight

"Now that we have a spy in Winslow, we may be getting closer to solving the mystery," I say as we pull out of the Mexicali Bistro's parking lot.

Ruger doesn't respond. I glance at the rider's side and see her stoically staring forward.

"Something bothering you? Was it the salad?"

Her eyes momentarily met mine before I turned my attention back to the road.

"Yeah, I didn't like you referring to me as your girlfriend."

I puffed a laugh. "Oh, that. What was I supposed to say to that hostess that we were cops investigating a murder?"

"What's wrong with that?"

I sigh, thinking it was better working with Kowalski. I didn't have to worry about hurt feelings. "Listen," I begin, "I'm trying to keep as low of a profile as possible and not have too many people talking about what we are doing. They might talk to the wrong person, and that person might make a seemingly innocuous comment to the wrong person. Right now, our suspects don't know we know some of the players. I want to keep it that way. Do you understand?"

With a huff, she says, "Yeah. I suppose you're right."

"We told Cassie not to breathe a word about the case and to let us know if they show up again. Right now, that's our ace in the hole."

"I don't want to have the same situation as I had in Phoenix."

I slowed down before making a right turn onto Highway 40.

"What happened in Phoenix?"

She appeared hesitant. "Okay, I'll tell you, but this doesn't go further than us—not even Kowalski. Got that?"

I nod. "You have my word."

"I won't bore you with the nitty-gritty details, but suffice it to say, there was a supervisor who had some interest in me. He was okay as a friend, but in my view, he was nothing more than that. He became aggressive, and when I was up for a raise, he held up that promotion, wanting more than I could give him ... if you know what I mean."

I made my way onto the freeway. "So, your response was to quit and move to Flagstaff?"

"In a nutshell? Yes."

I set the car's speed on the cruise control and eased back in my seat. "Your story isn't anything new. It happens all the time, not only in our business but in the private sector. Ah ... didn't that situation pose a problem when you applied for this job?"

"I was lucky. The deputy chief's wife was a friend of mine, and she talked with her husband on my behalf. The fact that it involved a lieutenant with political links complicated the situation. Anyway, here I am."

"Your story is safe with me."

"Oh, there's one more thing. I didn't want to destroy your fabricated fairytale about our relationship—I didn't say this in front of our waitress."

"What's that?"

"I enjoy drawing. There are those who consider my art very good. I have some on display in Sedona."

"You are full of surprises, aren't you?"

"I only mention that because when Cassie meets with us tomorrow, I can draw a picture of our mystery man with the help of the sketch-book guide."

"She will probably ask me why I brought my girlfriend to work."

"Very funny, Detective Owens."

Chapter Forty-Nine

Doug sits nervously in the interrogation room after being led there by a uniformed police officer. His eyes dart from one unadorned wall to the next, seeing nothing except a mirrored window and the door he came through. He tries pushing against the chair, hoping to rock it back, but finds it's secured to the concrete floor. He thinks back to the day he received a fifty-dollar bill as a tip and how his life went from bad to worse.

Doug stiffens as the door opens and sees Detective Owens give him a stern once-over. Detective Ruger follows him, the same detective who came to his apartment with Owens. She holds a large paper bag. They both move to the opposite side of the table and take their seats. Ruger places the bag on the floor between her and Detective Owens.

Detective Owens is the first to speak. "Doug McGuire, have you received your Miranda Rights?"

"Yes."

Owens continues. "Mr. McGuire, you already know my assistant, Detective Ruger. She will be taking notes while I ask you a few questions. You are being charged with the murder of Mr. Cody Dosela."

Doug shouts, "I didn't kill him. My friend Ralph Tyler and I saw him alive when we left Two Guns around six yesterday evening."

"An Arizona highway patrol officer saw you and your friend at the scene of the murder."

"We were there, but Cody was still alive when we left. I swear. Ask Ralph—he'll verify what I just said."

"We will. What were you doing there in the first place?"

"Listen, this is going to sound stupid, but we were looking for buried treasure. We got there early in the morning. We had a map ... I mean, some numbers ... Cody knew what they meant."

"You mean this?" Owens reaches into the bag, retrieves a clear evidence envelope with the matchbook cover inside, and sets it before Doug."

"Yeah, that's it."

"And, Mr. McGuire, where did you get that?"

Doug crosses his arms and casts his eyes down in front of him.

Owens, his voice rising, says, "Mr. McGuire, where did you get that?"

Doug's face burns red. "I got it from a hotel guest."

Owens slams his fist on the desk. "Who, Mr. McGuire? Who gave you this?"

"Sam Jackson."

"The same Samuel Jackson who was murdered in the hotel where you are employed as a night clerk?"

"Yes," Doug says, his voice almost at a whisper.

"So, don't you think it a strange coincidence that a man is killed in your hotel and another man dies because of some association with this?" Owens taps the sealed envelope.

"I didn't kill anyone."

Again, Detective Owens reaches into the bag and pulls out another clear evidence envelope, this time with a key inside. "And what about this?"

Doug shakes his head. "I haven't a clue."

"Okay, Mr. McGuire, why did you leave Mr. Cody Dosela?"

"It was getting dark. Cody told us to leave because we were done for the day. He had to pack all his stuff into his Bronco."

"Mr. McGuire, you said you arrived early in the morning, and according to your admission, you left near sunset. Is that correct?"

"Yes."

"That's a lot of time," says Detective Owens. "So, what did you accomplish?"

"Honestly, I'm not sure. Cody was writing stuff on a geographical map of some kind. I saw some of his marks. They appeared to cross an area a little south of the interstate."

"We were not able to find such a map. Do you know what happened to it?"

Doug shrugs. "I don't know. Cody says we had to come back again with a metal detector to try to find the treasure."

"Did you know they recovered a metal detector when the highway patrol found him?"

"What? Cody said he'd have to come back again, getting one from home."

Owens says, "I guess he was going to double-cross you."

Detective Emily Ruger, who had been taking notes, remained silent during the interview, jerks her head to attention.

Owens asks, "Mr. McGuire, how many guns do you own?"

"One—a Harrington & Richardson .22 caliber revolver."

"Did you have it with you when you were working with Mr. Dosela?"

"Yes."

Detective Owens asks, "Why, Mr. McGuire?"

"I ... I guess, we didn't trust him."

"When you say that you didn't trust him, did you think he might steal the treasure from you?"

"Yes."

Owens yells, "So, then you killed him—right."

McGuire, in tears, bawls, "No, a thousand times, no!"

Chapter Fifty

After sending McGuire back to his cell, Detective Ruger and I took a break before tackling the interview with Ralph Tyler. As we walked into the interrogation room, Tyler seemed laid back, unlike McGuire's edginess.

Ruger and I resumed our sitting positions, me on Tyler's right side and Ruger on his left. Again, like the last interview, Ruger places the evidence bag between us.

I begin, "Good afternoon, Mr. Tyler. I am Detective Owens, and this is Detective Ruger. Mr. Tyler, do you know why you are here?"

"Like, man, I don't know what this is all about. You guys read me the Five-O crap about my rights. Shouldn't I have a mouthpiece present?"

"Do you want a lawyer, Mr. Tyler?" asks Ruger.

"Nah, why do I need one? I'm in-o-sent."

"You do know that Mr. Cody Dosela was killed at Two Guns, don't you? I say, keeping a close watch on his reaction.

He moves uneasily in his chair. "Kiss my wrist. You ain't gonna pin that rap on me?"

I ask, "You do know him?"

"Yah, yah, I know him, but we weren't like buds. We were hangin' out most of yesterday. It doesn't mean I iced him."

"What were you doing with Mr. Dosela?"

"We were hunting for buried booty," he said, laughing.

"Why was Mr. Dosela with you and Mr. McGuire?"

"He was odd, you know. But he had the scope and all that crap. We were stoked about findin' our ticket outta here."

Ruger asks, "Do you own a gun, Mr. Tyler?"

"Yeah, a street howitzer."

"Excuse me?" asks Ruger while giving me a puzzled look.

Under my breath, I say to Ruger, "It's a shotgun."

"Did you use it recently?"

"Hell, no. Like, I don't remember the last time I did. Like it's probably not even yako."

I ask, "Mr. Tyler, when was the last time you saw Mr. Dosela?"

"It was ... past happy hour ... around six."

Responding to the knock on the door, I turn to my left to see a uniformed officer enter.

"I'm sorry for the interruption, but I have a call waiting for Detective Ruger. He says it was important."

Ruger gives me a look of bewilderment. I nod my consent for her to leave.

Knowing our interrogation was being recorded, I had no qualms about doing the interview solo.

"Mr. Tyler, how long have you known Doug McGuire?"

"We've been peeps since HS."

"Since your friendship goes back to high school, that makes you two really thick, doesn't it, Mr. Tyler?"

"Guess so."

"Enough to lie for?"

"Hold on, man. I know what you're trying to do. Listen, we didn't smoke, Cody. That's no lie."

"Okay, let's say you didn't kill Cody Dosela. Seeing you didn't find the treasure you were after, what was the plan?"

"I hadda work the next day. Me and Doug ask Cody if we could hit it hard next week Saturday. He says, okay. That's it. Doug drops me at my crib, and he goes to his pad. That's it—scouts honor." Pledge-like, Tyler holds up his right hand.

"Did you—"

The door of the interrogation room unexpectedly swings open. With determined steps, Ruger enters and immediately resumes her place next to me. She cups her hand over her mouth and whispers into my ear. "Come with me."

Curious, I follow her outside.

She closed the door behind us and says, "I just got off the phone with a Stewart Conservation Camp's filing clerk."

"And?"

"When I got the initial prison record of Paul Grendon, it didn't include the stuff from the Northern Nevada Correctional Center."

Frustrated with her theatrical suspense, I say, "Go on."

"You're not going to believe this."

"All right, already, get out with it."

"Our Mr. Grendon was a former employee of the CIA."

Chapter Fifty-One

After receiving the ballistics report from the Arizona Department of Public Safety, we had to release both Doug McGuire and Ralph Tyler. The report showed that Cody Dosela was killed with a 9mm, which matched the one used to kill Samuel Jackson, aka Oscar Burrows, and Paul Grendler. Before releasing them, Detective Ruger and I met them in the processing room.

Both men's eyes were downcast when we entered. Part of me felt a little sorry for each of them because they would have to explain their absence to their employers, albeit only for a day.

I began, "You two were damn lucky you didn't end up in the same meat wagon your friend Cody Dosela did. And you, McGuire, are lucky I don't book you for obstruction of justice."

"Ah—"

"Don't even try to justify holding back information, McGuire. If you say one more word, I will charge you for your lack of cooperation and withholding evidence. I advise you to can it. Do you understand?"

McGuire's head rocked like a bobblehead doll.

"Ralph Tyler half raised his hand. "Hey, man, ah, do you suppose we can still hunt for that buried booty?"

My disbelief at the question resulted in a delayed response.

Having already shown her ability for a quick rejoinder, Ruger says, "You realize that three people have already died because of this treasure?"

"Three?" exclaims McGuire.

Having recovered from the audacity of Tyler's question, I say, "Yep, your hotel guest, your uninvited night visitor, and, of course, your pal."

"That guy who came to my apartment is dead, too?" asks McGuire. "I didn't see anything in the papers about it."

"You wouldn't have. Paul Grendon, that's the guy who threatened you, didn't have any local connections. We asked the press not to publish the death. We knew it was a hit job, so we were more concerned about panicking the public."

"Hey man, so it's all right to resume the hunt?" asks Tyler.

Ruger shook her head. "Either you're not listening to us or just plain stupid. Search the entire desert, for all we care, but watch your backs. I'm done talking."

Before leaving, I add my advice. "You heard Detective Ruger. Now, after you sign out and get your belongings, take off. And one more thing. If you get followed or feel threatened, let us know while you still can."

* * *

Ruger and I return to our office to discuss the possibility of CIA involvement in the case.

"Boy, those are a pair," says Ruger.

"From my New York City experience, I've seen them all—stupid is stupid, no matter the location. Now, was the clerk from the Stewart Conservation Camp able to give you any more information about Paul Grendon and his job with the CIA?"

Ruger shook her head. "No, nothing more than that. Understanding their mission and the agency's secrecy, I doubt we can get any information from them."

"Like me, you're new to this area, but when you worked in Phoenix, didn't you hear any rumors about them?"

"I do remember something," says Ruger. "One of the guys down there shouts out to another detective, 'Are there still spooks in Luke?'"

"That's it?" I ask.

"Yeah. I don't remember if there was even a reply. I did hear that the Air Force is planning to receive F-16 jets at Luke Air Force Base, but that hasn't anything to do with what we are talking about."

"I'll tell you something I know from my time in New York. I heard this from a New York City police captain. He told me that the CIA has a liaison with the military. Basically, it's their taxi service."

"It's probably more than that, but it makes sense," says Ruger. "But aren't we getting off track?"

"We are. I think I know who can answer all our questions about the CIA."

"Who's that?"

I answer, "Kowalski. He's my local historian. I think he would appreciate a visit from us."

Chapter Fifty-Two

Although the streets of Flagstaff were free of ice and snow, the winter chill was still near fifty degrees for mid-February. Normally, we would have taken an unmarked police vehicle. Still, because our assigned car was undergoing routine maintenance and the backup was also out of commission, we had no other option but to use our privately owned vehicles.

Ruger walks out into the cold air and says, "You drove last. We can take my car."

I didn't want to be too brusque. So, I tempered my response. "Thanks anyway, but you've been working pretty hard on this case, and I think you deserve to take a break."

Getting into my Chevy Caprice, Ruger says, with a hint of sarcasm, "You're not one of those guys intimidated by a woman driver, are you?"

I laugh. "No. Your women's lib baiting won't work on me. It's more about legroom. Your Honda Civic doesn't have the legroom."

As we pulled out of the police station's parking lot, she asks, "On a related subject, what does a He-Man like you do when you're not chasing killers?"

"Why do you need to know that?"

"I'm just curious. I told you what I do on my off time. What's your secret life outside the force?"

"Okay, I'll tell you under the same conditions you placed on me."

"That's fair. It will be a mutual destruction pact. I can live with that."

"I enjoy going to my apartment and having a scotch or two."

Ruger squeals, "That's not fair. That's like saying I go home and have a drink, leaving out the drink and the rest of the sixteen hours. Come clean."

"That was just a tease. I knew you would react that way. Okay, after my liquid refreshment, I do some baking."

Ruger laughed uncontrollably. "You know what?"

"What?" I ask, already regretting the pact.

"That was never on my list of things I imagined you did in your free time."

"Before I go any further, what kinda stuff did you think I did?"

"Make model planes, write crime novels, go skiing, go fishing, or like Howard Hughes, sit around in your pajamas watching television with tissue boxes for slippers."

"Wow, I see. I'll have to work on my public image."

"I also thought you might be a knitter, but never a baker. Does Kowalski know about your secret life?"

I was expecting her to double down on the jokes about my hobby. Seeing her genuine interest, I open up. "No. I was afraid he would want me to make my own meals instead of him and his wife, Mary, inviting me for dinners."

"Very shrewd. Like, what do you bake?"

"Having lived in New York City most of my adult life, I miss the Jewish bakeries. When I relocated to Flagstaff, I had no idea the baked goods department lacked diversity. That's when I decided to make my own babka."

"What's babka?"

"It's a Jewish braided sweet bread that originated in Poland."

"Braided?"

"It's kinda hard to explain. Anyway, it's sweet, chocolatey, and delicious."

"Well, congratulations."

"Not so fast on the congrats. It took me several bags of flour before being satisfied with the results."

"Why didn't you ever bring any into work?" asks Ruger.

"What and have the nickname, doughboy or worse?"

She laughs, turns away, and looks at the passing scenery.

We spend the rest of the trip in uneasy silence until I break the quietness. "Here we are, Stan's little bit of paradise."

"He has a marvelous place," says Ruger, her eyes checking every inch of the building.

"His wife, Mary, was the driving force in building their new home. She didn't want Stan to constantly do repairs on the old house. So, anticipating retirement someday, they came up with this."

"I love the rustic knotty pine siding style, with heavy beams and log supports for the veranda. I bet it cost some to build it."

"Kowalski's hobby is woodworking. He did a lot of the work on the place, and he and his wife saved their money so they could afford it. Now, wait until you see the inside. That's where most of his talent is on display."

Chapter Fifty-Three

Kowalski, who sported an oxygen nasal cannula under his nose, greeted Ruger and me with his customary good-natured smile. He looked thinner than I had seen him last.

"Come on in. I just got up from my afternoon nap," he says, which accounts for the sleepy look on his face.

I notice Ruger's mien, wide-eyed and open-mouthed, as she gazed at the living room's beamed ceiling.

"Mary is out shopping."

That was good news for me, dodging a possible censure from her and the bad influence I had on Stan.

"Before this," Stan points to his oxygen appendage, "the two of us would go together. Now she saves money, not having me pick out the bad food choices, according to the doctor, that contributed to my health issues."

Ruger says, "Owens said you built this house yourself."

"C'mon, have a seat," says Kowalski, directing us into the step-down living room.

Ruger and I moved to the couch nearest the stone façade fireplace.

Kowalski pointed to the ceiling. "That was something I needed help with. Neither I nor my boys could have handled that big of a project."

"Well, I love the place," says Ruger, taking the spot closest to the hearth.

Kowalski selects the couch opposite. "So, is this a business or a pleasure visit?"

I say, "How are you doing before I tell you the reason?"

"The doc thinks I can return to work in about three weeks."

"That's good news, isn't it?" I ask.

"Yeah, but our plans for a trip to Rome and the Vatican will have to be postponed. Okay, now tell me why you're here."

"A surveyor by the name of Cody Dosela was found dead at Two Guns. He and Doug McGuire, along with his friend Ralph Tyler, were out there looking for buried treasure."

I unzip my down-filled jacket and pull out the evidence envelope from the Jackson case. "Here, have a look at this."

Kowalski looks at the contents of the clear plastic envelope and asks, "What am I looking at?"

"I got that stuff from Doug McGuire. The numbers on the matchbook cover are coordinates marking the position of buried treasure for the Wells Fargo stagecoach robbery in 1881."

Kowalski's eyes light up. "Really?"

"I can't say, but three people died because of this."

Kowalski grabs the key within the packet. "And what's this all about?"

"I haven't the slightest idea. You can see by the stamping that it was manufactured by the Francis Keil & Sons Company. I conducted some research and discovered that they were founded in 1876. We went to the Weatherford Hotel and thought we could find room 209."

"And?" asks Kowalski.

"Room 209 is now part of room 203."

Kowalski says, "You do know that the Weatherford wasn't the only hotel in Flagstaff around that time. The Madison Building was built around 1887 or 1888, I'm not sure—predates the Weatherford by almost ten years."

I ask, "And they had a hotel in that building?"

"Yep. It had a bank was on the first floor, and the hotel on the second floor. You can see for yourself. I think the original builder, Madison, left out the 'and' as a cost saver. Anyway, that's my spin on it."

Ruger, who had been preoccupied with admiring the room, turned to Kowalski and asks, "What's the name of the bank?"

"Yeah, know, I don't think people look up that much at buildings anymore. It says Wells Fargo Hotel." He laughed. "That's the rub."

Ruger, continues. "Flagstaff has a lot of historical buildings that are nearly untouched since being built, with the exception of the Weatherford Hotel. Maybe the real key, no pun intended, is that building?"

My mind raced. "The train robbery occurred in 1889. The Weatherford was constructed around 1897, and the Madison around 1887. So, the actual place of interest must be the hotel."

I notice Ruger glance at her watch. She tapped its surface.

Rising from the couch, I say, "Stan, we really have to get going. We have a ten o'clock appointment with a waitress who can possibly identify the companion of our mystery woman with the chunky lightning bolt ring."

Kowalski says, "I'm jealous, missin' all the excitement of this case."

"Get well soon. Maybe you can help us put this to bed when you get back."

Chapter Fifty-Four

Cassie was only a few minutes late. We took her to the integration room only because it offered the most privacy. At first, she appeared confused when she saw Ruger. She says nothing, despite my "girlfriend" remark in the restaurant, and doesn't bring up the matter. Ruger laid down the forensic art composite book and her drawing sketchpad on the metal table that separated us. Cassie took a position next to Ruger on the interrogator's side while I sat across from them.

Ruger began, "You said in the restaurant that the man was round-faced?"

"Yes," Cassie answers nervously.

I stepped in. "Cassie, I want you to relax. There's no incorrect answer. Just tell Detective Ruger what you remember."

I could see Cassie's shoulders drop.

Ruger pointed to four facial styles ranging from fat to muscular. "Which one looks the closest to the man's face?"

She points. "That one, the third one from the left."

Ruger draws an oval outline. She then crosses the outline with proportional horizontal and vertical lines.

"Now, what about the eyes? Look at these ten samples."

Cassie points to the small, round-shaped eyes.

"Now we'll try the nose." Ruger flipped a page. "Do any of these look like the man's features?"

Without hesitation, she points to the sharp, pointed nose.

Ruger starts to draw in the nose, but Cassie says, "No, not that much, just a little shorter nose."

Ruger erases part of the nose.

"Yes, that's better."

When it came to the lips, Cassie says, "He had a slight hairlip, but overall, his lips were long and tight."

Ruger sketches.

"Yes, like that."

"Now, let's try the mustache."

Before Ruger could ask the question, Cassie exclaims, "That one right there, the Joseph Stalin mustache, only it didn't cover his upper lip that much."

Ruger sketches and, after a bit, asks, "And the cheeks?"

"He had kinda a full face, not fat, just kinda substantial."

By the time Ruger finished the drawing, the depiction looked so realistic that Cassie gasped, saying, "That's him, that's him. Wow."

When we finished, we thanked her for her time and cautioned her not to do anything rash, but to immediately call us if he or Valerie Vaughn should ever show up in her restaurant again.

I added my advice. "If they should show up, be very discreet. Make the call and try to act nonchalant. We'll handle the rest."

Once Cassie was on her way, Ruger held up the sketch and says, "Not bad, hey?"

I say, "Suitable for framing. Now, all we have to do is make copies and circulate them among our patrols. And seeing that Winslow may be their base of operation, we should give their police department a few copies as well."

"It's almost one o'clock, and I'm famished. Do you suppose we could take a break?" bemoans Ruger.

"Sounds good," I say. "It's past the lunch rush. So, let's go to Mr. Bob's."

"Do they have my kind of food?"

"As a matter of fact, they do. They are vegetarian-friendly, but I hope you don't mind if I sink my teeth into one of their famous cheeseburgers?"

Ruger mocks, "Go ahead. It's your arteries."

"Then I suppose you won't be having one of their pies, *a la mode*?"

"Sorry to disappoint your fun, but I love pies and ice cream, especially when they are together."

Chapter Fifty-Five

Although Mr. Bob's was a little out of the way, both Ruger and I agreed our meals were satisfying, so much so that I was inclined to take a nap. While I now agree with the logic of the siesta, we made our way to the Madison building, fighting the notion.

After a stretch of silence, Ruger says, "This whole situation is a bit confusing to me. Let me get this straight again: the train robbery occurred in 1889, and the Weatherford was constructed around 1897, but the Madison building was around 1887. While we have been concentrating on the Weatherford, the actual place of interest has to be the Madison Hotel."

"Yeah, it's beginning to look that way."

"Okay, but bear with me a minute," she says while opening up her notebook.

"Go ahead."

Ruger begins. "There seems to be a lot of moving parts to this story. Some of them are not making any sense."

"Like what?" I ask.

"The train robbery occurred in 1889, and the Madison Hotel was built in 1888."

"Go on."

"Now, the five robbers made their way to the hideout. According to my research, they didn't have time to check into a hotel, somehow hide the loot, and then hightail it to Veit Springs. It's out of the way."

I ask, "Where do you think they hid the treasure?"

"It has to be somewhere in or around Two Guns. According to witnesses, they only had horses, and the amount of gold and silver would have slowed them down. So, it's only logical."

"What are you getting at?"

"The matchbook with the numbers and the key to room 209 are two separate issues."

"Honestly, that's the same thing that bothers me, too."

* * *

I eased my car next to the Madison Building. We walked to the corner of the building that bordered the old Highway 66, across from the train station. I tried the door without success and then cupped my hand over my forehead and peered inside the door's window. The interior appeared to be unoccupied except for a collection of boxes and an eclectic assortment of furnishings.

Ruger gestured. "We passed a side entrance."

"Yeah, I thought this place was open and would know more about the building."

We backtracked to the side entrance, opened the door, and went to the second floor. My spirits brightened when I saw the numbering on each door while Ruger paced up and down the hallway and scanned each entrance.

She looks puzzled, saying, "There isn't a room 209."

"Yeah. It's obvious that rooms 208 and 210 once bordered 209." I tried the door. "Okay, let's see who's home. "I opened door number 210.'

An attractive young girl with a Janet Jackson-style wild hairdo faced the entrance and looked up from her desk. She gives us a forced smile and considers us with apprehension. "Good afternoon," she says, leaning back in her chair.

I return the greeting and produce my badge. "I am Detective

Owens, assisted by Detective Ruger. We are with the Flagstaff Police Department and are investigating a murder which occurred several weeks ago."

Her demeanor stiffened. "I know nothin' about a murder in this building," she says, her voice taut.

"It wasn't here, but our investigation believes the office space between you and the adjacent workplace may offer a clue."

The young girl leans forward on her desk. "To the best of my knowledge, that room is used as storage space. Although I can't say for certain because I don't have any way to get in there—I don't think anyone's been in there since I started working here."

I ask, "Who do you send the rent to?"

"Sure, I can help you with that. Here, I'll write the address on the back of our business card."

She jots down the information and hands me her card. "I see they're on Aspen Avenue."

"Yes, sir. They are just a couple of blocks down. Once in a while, I even skip mailing in the payment and go for a walk there instead. Is there anything else I can help you with?" she asks, the tension clearly gone.

"Actually," I scan the desk for a name, "um, there is." I hold up the key." Without a warrant, I can't open the door down the hall. I would like you to come with us and witness us trying this key."

Obviously, sensing my curiosity, she says, "By the way, my name is Sally King."

Ruger extends a hand and says, "Pleased to meet you, Sally."

She says, "This is the most exciting thing that has happened to me since working here. Let's go."

I faced the nameless door. Detective Ruger stood on my right while Sally King took a position on my left. It became an eureka moment when the key slid into the keyway with barely any resistance. Turning it, my excitement turned to euphoria.

Chapter Fifty-Six

Sharon MacFarlane sat across from her desk, stern-faced, her eyes burrowing into Doug McGuire. "No phone call—nothing. I had to work a double shift. I could barely stay awake. What's your excuse for not showing up yesterday?"

Doug, his eyes cast down in embarrassment, raises them but avoids her menacing stare. "I was arrested."

"What? Speeding or something? You weren't drunk, were you?"

Doug hesitates. "I-um-it was for murder."

"Murder? Who did you kill, and how come you aren't still in jail?"

"I didn't kill anyone. It was a big mix-up?"

"Well, who died?"

"He was sort of a friend of my buddy, Ralph. We were the last people to see him."

"Who was it?" she asks, leaning forward on her desk.

"You don't know him. His name is Cody Dosela." Once more, Doug's eyes study the floor.

Seemingly perplexed by his evasiveness, Sharon appears to vacillate between anger and sympathy. "Who all knows about this? It's not going to be in the papers, is it?"

"I don't think so. There weren't any reporters."

"That doesn't mean anything," she shrieked. "I can't have a murder suspect working in this hotel. Think about the PR."

"I didn't kill anyone. Sharon, I need this job. The economy sucks, especially the gas situation, and I barely make enough to live on. Did you see the morning paper?"

"No. Stay here. They usually drop off a stack about now," she says, bolting out of the office.

Sharon returns almost as fast as she left. She unfolds the paper, feverishly scanning the front page before moving on. Now, the paper becomes a curtain of newsprint blocking Doug's view of her.

Doug nervously studies his moist hands. The rustling of paper amid Sharon's grunts unnerves him.

Finally, with a punctuated crush of paper, she cries, "Here it is." It's followed by a recital of garbled words. Apparently, coming to the end of the article, she folds the newspaper in one final act of relief and slaps it down on her desk. "We dodged the bullet," she says triumphantly.

"I take it my name wasn't mentioned?"

"No, it wasn't. Now, for both our sakes, don't share your knowledge of this Cody fella with any of our staff. Got that?"

"Yes, I understand," Doug says sheepishly.

"The article only says they found the body in Two Guns. Why is that?"

"I think the police want to keep a tight lid on it."

Sharon leans forward, resting her arms on the desk. "What were you doing in Two Guns?"

Doug exhales and hesitates.

"C'mon, out with it. I'm certainly not going to blab a word of this."

"We were hunting for buried treasure."

Doug expected her boisterous laugh and felt the warmth of his blush.

Chapter Fifty-Seven

As some of this puzzle fell into place, I became more confident that we were on the right track. As we searched for a judge, the dial on my watch seemed to race each time I glanced at it. Finally, with the warrant in hand, Ruger and I walk into the management company holding control over the Madison Building.

When I open the door, the two employees sitting at their desks look at us in annoyance, like clerks in a department store seeing a last-minute customer.

The one closest to us asks unenthusiastically, "How may I help you?"

I reply in my best impersonation of a clueless shopper, "I'm Detective Owens, and this is Detective Ruger of the Flagstaff Police Department. I hope we're not going to inconvenience you too much. We have a search warrant for room 209 in the Madison Building."

Previously sitting at her desk, she rises. "We are about to close. Does this have to be done tonight?"

Not wanting to sugarcoat our request, I reply, "Yes. This involves a murder investigation, and time is of the essence. We don't need your entire staff. Only one representative from your company will suffice."

"My name is Shaylee, and I'm the office manager." She turns to the woman behind her and says, "Julie, you can take off. I'll handle this."

Julie scoffs. "You kidding me, Shaylee. A murder investigation, and you want me to go home?"

"Suit yourself."

Ruger chimes in, "Before we go, I would like to see all the information you have on that room—in particular, his or her name of the renter and mailing address."

Shaylee says, "I always suspected that something was not quite right." She moves to a file cabinet at the back of the office. "It was before my time, but that room and renter have the longest contract of all our clients." She opens the file drawer and fumbles for a folder at the rear of the drawer. "Here it is," she says triumphantly.

Detective Ruger takes the folder and opens it on Shaylee's desk. Retrieving two sheets of paper, she asks, "Is this all you have?"

"That would be correct, Detective. That was another reason for my suspicions."

"I see you collected eight hundred dollars a month starting in 1964, and the lease was for twenty years."

"Yes, it appeared to be straightforward—the amount and the time."

"I see that," Ruger remarks, "And paid in full, sixteen thousand dollars in cash."

I pick up the sheet. "A lot of red flags on this one and an address in Phoenix, to boot."

"I'm surprised that someone would agree to this," says Ruger. "The flat rate and the length. I mean, things can change, but the contract locks everything up for twenty years."

Julie speaks up, "In 1964, to get eight hundred dollars a month for a room, I would venture to say for a place that was hard to rent, was a deal for the company."

My curiosity rising, I ask, "Did anyone in your company attempt to contact this person?"

"I did, last year, "says Shaylee. "Seeing that we were coming to the end of the contract in a few years, and my own inquisitiveness, I sent a letter to that address. I thought it was a crafty way of satisfying my curiosity. The letter came back marked, "'Return to Sender.'"

I ask, "One more question before we go. Did either of you, or to the best of your knowledge, did anyone take a look-see in that room?"

Shaylee, says, "You probably didn't notice the fine print on the enclosed contract. It stipulates that if anyone were to enter that room without the renter's consent, all rent payments would revert to the renter. Suffice it to say, that was enough reason for us to abide by the agreement."

I joke, "Well, ladies, how about a ride?"

"As long as it isn't to jail," replies Julie.

* * *

The trip to the Madison Building didn't take long enough to even warm up our car.

As we begin our climb to the second floor, Shaylee exclaims, "Oh, we forgot the key. We'll have to go back to the office."

"It's not a problem," I answer. "I have one." Whereupon, both Shaylee and Julie give me a questioning glance.

The sun had set, leaving the floor illuminated only by four low-wattage bulbs evenly spaced along the ceiling. Passing Sally King's office, I notice the frosted glass on her door lacked light.

Holding the key in my hand and suspended in front of the keyway, I remark, "Now, we all are about to satisfy our curiosity."

I simultaneously turned the lock and doorknob, pushed my way in, and blindly reached for the wall switch. To my surprise, and confirmed by our group's collective gasp, the room was totally empty, even of the most basic furnishings.

Chapter Fifty-Eight

After dismissing Shaylee and Julie, Ruger and I examined every inch of the flooring and walls. We were confident we would find something that warranted an eight-hundred-dollar-a-month, twenty-year lease.

"I feel like a mime," says Ruger as she feels her way along the entire length of the wall.

"We have been frisking these walls and old-fashioned knockin' at least three times, and frankly, my arms are getting tired and my knuckles sore," I said, partly out of frustration and partly as a joke.

Ruger laughs and begins moving her arms mime-like over nonexistent walls.

"Yeah, I got it," I say in agreement with her mocking gestures. "Let's call it a night."

"Sounds good to me. Yeah, know, it's possible that whatever you think might be in this room is long gone."

"You might be right. I'm thinking differently right now because of the lease's length. Maybe there was something here at one time. Or, someone intended to come back well into the future—perhaps when things cooled down."

"And do what?" asks Ruger.

"I don't know."

"What's the plan?" she asks.

"Tomorrow, we'll contact the Arizona Department of Public Safety and let them have a go at it. In the meantime, let's follow up on the address associated with this room. No one rents something without providing some form of identification such as a name, address, or other personal information. The other possibility is that maybe the person who rented this place died, which is why the letter was returned?"

"Sounds plausible," says Ruger.

I ask, "Maybe you can check into that tomorrow?"

"Sure thing." She clears her throat. "Not that you're answerable to me, but what will you be doing?"

"Once we connect with the state's forensics department, I'll meet with them here and let them in. Then fill Kowalski in on what we found so far. I hate bothering him, but he does know a lot about this area. Besides, I think it's a morale booster for him."

"I can tell," says Ruger. "He sure perked up when we visited him last."

"It's a morale booster for me, too. Anyway, let's wrap this up. I'm getting tired."

"What, so you can go home and bake something?"

I laugh. "Ha, ha. No, so I can have my scotch and go to bed."

* * *

I drop off Ruger at the station so she could pick up her Honda Civic, then made a beeline to my place. Sometimes, those stairs to my place felt like I was climbing Mount McKinley. After spending more than enough time in a cramped vehicle or stale office, the welcome freshness of my place was a reward in itself. My next reward was behind the two doors of my liquor cabinet, which I enthusiastically opened before reaching for my bottle of Macallan scotch, my choice for special occasions—this being one of those moments.

With a double dose of comfort in my glass, I move to my stereo, select some soothing music, and then nest myself in my easy chair. My respite was short-lived when, out of the corner of my eye, I notice the blinking red light near my phone. Being a cop, one never ignores the metaphorical holler of an answering machine. Setting my drink aside, I go to check out the message.

I push the play button. "Hi, Jack. This is Babs. Call me when you get this message. Don't worry about the time ... " She gives me the number, then a beep.

I glance at my watch and see it's a bit shy of eight p.m., which means it's almost ten in New York City.

I dial the number, and on the second ring, Babs picks up. "Hello?" she answers, her voice stiff.

"Babs, this is Jack. You asked me to call you?"

She sniffled. "Yeah. It's Jessica ... she passed this morning," Babs bawls. Even over the phone, Jack could hear attempts to control herself. She divulges through starts and stops of anguished-filled words, "She ... she ... wanted to call you ... at the ... end."

A lump forms in my throat. "She told me two months ago that she was going to start treatments for her cancer?"

"Jack, she was diagnosed ... with cancer ... five years ago," Babs says, followed by a gush of weeping.

"She never said anything to me about that."

"Our trip to Flagstaff ... that was her last goodbye."

I waited for something else to say, but words evaded me.

"Jack, do you think you'll be able ... to attend the funeral?"

Grief paralyzed me.

"Jack?" Babs asks in mournful supplication.

Breaking out of my stupor, I say, "No, I can't. I'm involved in a big case."

"Yeah, ah ... I'll send you the funeral arrangements when I hear more. Good night, Jack," Babs signs off, followed by a click.

Now, it was my turn to cry.

Chapter Fifty-Nine

Ruger greets me with her usual frivolity as she rounds the corner into the office. "Morning, Jack. Ready to break this case wide open?" she says, then takes a sip of tea from her mug.

My lack of a restful night and emotional strain prevented me from being chipper in my response. Instead, it was monotone, lacking a reciprocal glee. "Ready as I'll ever be. I'll call the Public Safety guys to set up a time for us to meet at the Madison Building. Like I said yesterday, you do the research on that renter."

Probably sensing my lack of enthusiasm, she asks, "What, all the excitement of maybe closing this case is leaving you with post-event letdown syndrome? I understand it can happen to athletes, too."

I had to give her an explanation. "When I got home, there was a message on my machine. It was from my former wife's friend, Babs. She told me that my wife had just died."

Ruger's cheerfulness evaporated. "Oh, I'm sorry to hear that," she says sincerely, holding out her hand. "Accept my condolences."

I take her hand in mine. "Thank you. We divorced six years ago but remained in touch, on and off, during that time." I let go of Ruger's hand, which I thought was surprisingly warm, considering the chill in the squad room.

Ruger says, "Understandably, you probably don't want to discuss it. You're going to do your thing, and I'll be busy with mine."

I nod, pick up the phone off my desk, and dial. After shuffling between three different departments and explaining the uniqueness of my request, I finally connected with the right person. Honestly, I was grateful for the diversion, which helped me detach myself from the sorrow I was experiencing. Although at this point my involvement was simply as a facilitator, the mystery held me captive, and I wanted answers.

* * *

Leaving Ruger busy with her research, I got into my car and drove to the Madison Building. Yesterday, while traveling back to the station, I noticed a new coffee shop that had sprung up along Beaver Street. Figuring my wait was a given, and my eagerness to get out of the office, coupled with the forensics team's vague promise of their arrival time, I'd give the place a try.

My olfactory sensitivities awoke the minute I entered. As a coffee connoisseur who misses the options of New York City, the place was a welcome discovery and momentary diversion. Taking my order, I returned to my car, where my thoughts of Jessica greeted me.

With the warmth of coffee to keep me company, I pulled in front of the side entrance and leaned back to wait for the team's arrival. Although I was eager to see what they would find, if anything, I welcomed peace and solitude. Alone in meditation, my thoughts of Jessica played like a love story in my mind early in our marriage. Eventually, it all came crashing down when our careers took precedence.

Despite the jolt of caffeine, I drifted off until I awoke from my slumber by the tapping on the driver's side window. I glanced at my watch and saw I had dozed off for nearly an hour. I open the door and step outside.

"You must be Detective Owens?" says the man in a one-piece blue coverall. "I'm Tim Dutton. I see you took advantage of us being late."

We shake hands. 'Yep, I had a restless night. I see there are only two of you."

"Yeah. My partner Pete and I were told it wasn't a crime scene. All you needed was a sounding scan of the walls, ceiling, and floor."

"Basically, that's it," I say, checking out Pete as he removes some equipment cases from the crime lab's station wagon. "I have a feeling, call it cop intuition, that something's hidden somewhere in that room."

"I love a good treasure hunt," says Dutton. "Let's do this."

I lead while Dutton and his partner, Pete, follow me. Having traveled this staircase yesterday, I quickly noticed traces of plaster embedded in the stair treads. I began to have a sinking feeling in my stomach that something was amiss. Rounding the corner on the second floor, I rushed to room 209, where the lock had been forced. Pushing the door open, the telltale cavity on the wall told me we were beaten to whatever was there yesterday.

Tim says, "So, I guess this is now a crime scene?"

I nod.

Chapter Sixty

I left the Madison Building and the crime lab boys to do their stuff. This new turn of events crowded out Jessica's death. I began to beat myself up over my carelessness by not considering the possibility of being tailed. Right now, I need a friend and guidance. Kowalski checked both of those boxes.

Mary Kowalski greets me at the door. Although civil, I saw a hint of suspicion in her eyes. "Hi, Jack." She says in a monotone greeting. "Stan's just getting up from a nap. C'mon in and make yourself comfortable in front of the fireplace."

By the time I reached the couch, Stan had entered the family room. "You're looking good," I say, checking my descent onto the sofa.

With his usual robust welcome, he takes my hand and says, "Maybe I should be getting back to the office so you wouldn't have to come so far each day?"

We both laugh. "I don't think Mary would like that idea," I say and resume my attempt to get comfortable on the couch.

Stan sits opposite me in what I assume was his avowed easy chair. "What's it this time?" he asks.

"I just came back from the Madison Building. I expected to find something hidden of value that would explain the twenty-year lease.

Instead, I was thumped by someone who broke into the place last night and found whatever was hidden in the walls."

Stan laughed so hard I was expecting to have another heart attack. "And you figured I had all the answers?"

"I figured you may have some of the answers."

Kowalski smiles and leans forward in his chair, almost as if he's going to tell me a secret without anyone in the empty room hearing. "Jack, you're a smart cop. You must realize by now you have two different cases that are muddling your mind."

"Yeah, I know that now," I admit.

"Okay," Stan begins, "You have two different time periods and they are not meshing. So, you have to treat each one on its own merits. It's going to be difficult, but you need to be focused. I think you are dealing with two treasures. The buried stagecoach robbery and the other one that I actually think is more current."

I nod. "And the key is we have two different prisoners, who through fate, were drawn together and probably hatched their plot while in stir."

"Now look at it from the perspective of the criminal mind," says Stan.

"That's actually easy," I say. "Greed is the great divider among felons. Every drug deal that goes bad has greed as its core."

Stan says, "Yeah, and that is probably why you have three deaths so far."

The sound of the doorbell distracted us.

Mary Kowalski comes to the door and answers it. Both Stan and I sit back and wait to see who's the caller.

Mary says, "Oh, it's Detective Ruger," as she holds open the door to let her in.

Ruger apologizes, "I'm sorry to interrupt, but I have some important information for Detective Owens."

"C'mon in," says Mary cheerfully, receiving Ruger with more cordiality than my greeting. Perhaps it was a female thing. "Can I get you something to drink?"

Ruger says, "I would appreciate a glass of water."

"Why don't you have a seat with the men as they plot something I'm not privy to," says Mary, and chuckles.

Ruger joins us, taking the same spot near the fireplace she had during her last visit. She says, "I first stopped at the Madison Building, and the guy in charge told me you left about half an hour ago. So, using my powers of deduction and your declaration of itinerary ... what can I say—here I am."

Kowalski laughs. "At least you keep better tabs on him than I did."

I said, "I told you where I was always going. You never paid attention. So, what's so important that you couldn't wait until I returned to the office?"

She reached inside her briefcase and pulled out several sheets of paper. "I figured both of you would want to hear this news."

I think Kowalski was just as excited by the tease as I was. "Okay, you got our attention," I said. "Out with it."

Ruger smoothed out a sheet of paper on her lap. "We know that Paul Grendon was an agent for the CIA. What we don't know is why he left their employment. It appears the CIA has a lot of cash used as payout money to individuals willing to sell information for a price. Those funds were given out like candy within the agency without much oversight or audit trail."

"Don't tell me," I say. "Grendon pocketed some of the cash?"

Ruger points to me and nods. "Give that man a kewpie doll."

"How much cash?" asks Kowalski.

"A cool million and a half. And based on my informant, chump change for the Government."

I reply, "I'm no math wizard, but I would guess the size of the holes in that room at the Madison Building was its repository until yesterday."

Chapter Sixty-One

Doug McGuire leaned over a worksheet behind the counter of the Double Six Hotel, unaware that Ralph Tyler hovered on the opposite side. Sensing a presence, Doug looks up and, with a start, shouts, "What the hell, Ralph! I'm on edge already, and you come sneaking in here like a killer."

Ralph laughs. "Cool it, man. I was only gonna jerk your chain. Don't be a 'spaz.'"

"Why are you here?"

"It's late. I didn't think you'd be too crazy with customers."

"Ralph, don't you have to work tomorrow?"

"I'm takin' what the man calls a 'personal day.' I call it a goof-off day."

"Okay. Again, why are you here?"

"I thought we'd shoot the bull and plan our next trip to Two Guns."

"Weren't you paying attention to what that cop said about a killer?"

"Listen, we go there in broad daylight, pack heat, and search for our ticket outta here."

Doug says, "Don't you remember what Cody said? We need a metal detector."

217

Ralph bends down, out of Doug's view, and then triumphantly brandishes the object of their desire. "Like this?"

"Where did you get that?"

"I borrowed it from the engineering department."

"You mean stole it," accuses Doug.

"Borrowed. It's stolen if I don't return it."

"Ralph, you got some balls. How long can we *borrow it*?"

"Til Monday."

Doug says, "So, we gotta use it on Saturday or Sunday? Ralph, I'm already in hot water. Saturday's a no-go, but I think I could manage to get off on Sunday. Let me see that geological map you waved around the other day."

"Say no more." Ralph pulls out a map from the inside pocket of his winter jacket.

"Where did—never mind, I don't want to know."

Ralph says, "C'mon over to my crib tomorrow afternoon, and we'll scope out the caper. Dig it?"

Doug laughs. "Yeah, I dig it."

Waving the metal detector in the air, Ralph says, "High-ho, Silver," as he heads for the door.

* * *

Doug knocks on Ralph's door loud enough, trying to overcome the television's cacophony of music and recognizable beeps of the Roadrunner. As if on cue, the noise abates enough for Doug to hear approaching footsteps.

Ralph, holding a can of beer in one hand and the remote control in the other, shouts, "Hey, man, how's it hanging?"

"Hey, Ralph," says Doug, his eyes squinting as if he could control the sound with them, "How's about cutting that volume down a notch or two so I can think?"

Ralph pirouettes, almost losing his balance, and shoots an invisible ray at the TV to muffle Bugs Bunny. "There, good buddy, done. Care for a brewski?"

"You bet. Some people might frown at seeing me soaking up the suds at nine in the morning, but we third shift people live differently than the rest of society."

"Right on, right on," Ralph concurs, while heading for the refrigerator.

Ralph sets the remote, along with his beer, on the kitchen counter and opens the refrigerator door. He pulls out a can of Schlitz, pops the sta-tab, and hands it to Doug.

Doug lifts the can in the air as a salute. "Thanks, pal," he says, making a glug-glug-glub noise as he downs the brew. He smacks his lips before letting go with a forceful belch.

Ralph laughs. "Bet you can't do that in your highfalutin hotel?"

"And why would I?" Doug answers with a smile.

"Doug, you need more lessons in cool."

They both laugh. Doug says, "Maybe you can pull yourself away from the Saturday morning cartoons, and we can get down to business."

"Aye, aye, Captain," he says, aiming and making sounds like he was shooting it with a Star Trek Phaser. He returns the remote to the counter and joins Doug at the kitchen table.

"Ralph, at the hotel, you evaded my question. Where did you get the map? Do you want to tell me now?"

"Why?" asks Ralph as he slides onto one of the storage bench seats.

"I just want to know," Doug replies, his voice rising.

"Cool your jets, man. When Cody started packing his stuff, I figured, since we were coming back, anyway...."

"That explains Cody's death."

"What you talking about?"

"You know what that means, Ralph?"

"Yeah. Like, he couldn't stiff us and lift it for himself."

"No, you idiot. He died because those people are after the treasure, too."

"Which means?"

"Which means we're still in their crosshairs."

Chapter Sixty-Two

Doug merges onto Highway 40 and heads east to Two Guns. Ralph, who has succumbed to the effects of his early morning can of beer, sleeps. Doug yawns, checks his watch, and sees it's 6:15. Estimating his travel time of nearly half an hour, he figures he will arrive about fifteen minutes before sunrise. He checks his rearview mirror, worried he may have someone following him. He thinks anyone interested in his destination will already know where he is going and will give him a wide berth. His apprehension increases. He fidgets, his palms moist with anxiety, and continues his obsession by glancing at the road ahead, followed by hurried glimpses in all mirrors. Ralph's snoring and the pressure of being followed heighten his annoyance.

Ralph begins to stir as Doug's AMC Pacer exits a smooth blacktop before going onto the rougher terrain of Two Guns. With a groggy utterance, he says, "We there already?"

"Yeah, Bud. We have arrived."

Ralph stretches and yawns while scanning the area. "It's still kinda dark, pal."

"Don't worry, it'll start to lighten up soon."

The car stops several yards to the west of the abandoned gas station.

With one hand on the door's handle, Ralph says, "I gotta pee."

The dome light makes Doug squint. "Just don't piss on my car," he says and straightens up before getting out himself. Following Ralph's need to relieve himself, he does the same.

"Hey, pal," Ralph calls out. "Maybe we're pissing on the treasure?"

"That's a thought," says Doug. "We'll see what the map says."

Finished, Doug goes to the rear of the Pacer, where Ralph joins him. He opens the trunk and says, "I'll feel a lot more comfortable if we keep your shotgun close by."

"I figured if we're gonna be into some hard-core shit, I'd get myself a box of buckshot for my street howitzer."

"How many rounds will it hold?" asks Doug.

"Five shells, man." He picks up the shotgun, aims it into the coming dawn, and yells, "Bang, bang, bang, bang. 'I know what you're thinking: did he fire five shots or only four?'"

"Okay, *Dirty Harry*, you got that *howitzer* loaded?"

"Comin' right up, man." Ralph opens the box of shells that sat on the trunk's flooring and pumps five rounds into the shotgun, one by one. He set the safety. "There, all ready for action. You got your piece ready, my main man?"

Doug taps the outside of his cargo jacket, indicating its readiness. "C'mon, Ralph, let's look at your map on the front of my car."

Ralph places the shotgun beside the pickaxe and other tools next to the metal detector.

"By the way, Ralph, where did you get all that digging equipment?"

"Like everything else, man, on loan." Ralph laughs.

Going to the front of the Pacer, Ralph unfolds the map and smooths it over the car's rounded hood. Holding a flashlight, Doug steadies its beam on the penciled X'd pattern.

Doug points to the map. "See this X, it's right about at the end of the old Highway 66. That makes sense because that part of 66 was torn up when they did Interstate 40."

Ralph asks, "What's your skinny on what happened?"

"Whoever wrote those numbers on the matchbook must have done it on the side so as not to arouse any suspicion. He must have been part of the survey crew. The guy figures he'll be back, but something happens."

"Maybe he was that dude who got offed in your roach motel?"

"We don't have any roaches in our place."

"Sorry 'bout that, man."

"Ralph, the cops probably know this shit—Jackson was going to meet someone, but he was double-crossed. I got the info about where the treasure was buried because he didn't trust anyone."

"He was covering his ass. Right, man?"

"Yeah," Doug agrees. "And they didn't know I had it."

"Hey, man, are we gonna jaw, or get our treasure?"

"Yeah, yeah. Let's move."

Ralph places the shotgun back into the trunk of the Pacer, then joins Doug on the front seat.

Doug, leaving the gas station behind him, eases the car along a gravel road. Approaching the junction that led to the Canyon Diablo Bridge, he stops. "Ralph, I'm gonna park on the opposite side of Highway 66, which will block the view of us digging."

"Roger that," says Ralph.

Doug turns to Ralph. "I don't think we're going to have a lot of time. You remember that cop who questioned us?"

"Yeah."

"Well, he or another cop probably will wanna see what we're doing. So, I don't want to explain myself. Got that?"

"Hey, man, I'm cool. You da boss."

Doug replies, "I'm not the boss. C'mon, let's make this happen."

"Cowabunga!"

Chapter Sixty-Three

I open the Flagstaff telephone directory. Between flipping through the business section, sipping my morning coffee at my desk, I find three listings for hardware stores. I jot down the names and addresses.

Detective Ruger, as usual, arrives on time, holding whatever health beverage she found appealing that morning. With her typical pleasantness, she says, "Morning, Detective Owens."

"Good morning to you, too," I reply sincerely, thinking we're on a fast track in solving this case.

"You're sounding pretty chipper," she says on the way toward her borrowed desk.

I say, "Where would you begin if you wanted to dig up buried treasure?"

She carefully sets her hot beverage on the desk, then eases herself into the chair. "Let see, you said buried, which would imply some digging. So, I would first go to the cemetery and steal a shovel."

I couldn't help but laugh. "Although that is a possible answer for a demented mind, I, on the other hand, would go to the hardware store and *buy* one."

"Ah, you are wrong, Sherlock. Maybe the person interested in finding the treasure doesn't want anyone to know about his or her intentions."

"Okay, I see your point. But for argument's sake, he isn't as sharp as you and unthinkingly goes to the hardware store and purchases one."

"Seeing Flagstaff has only three hardware stores, that should be easy."

I ask, "How do you know Flagstaff has only three hardware stores?"

With the arrogance of a know-it-all, she says, "Because they don't sell scotch in them. Therefore, you wouldn't know the number or location. On the other hand, because of my hobby as an artist, I often frequent them for supplies such as some paints, thinners, and wood for stretching canvas, *etcetera*."

"You haven't been in Flagstaff that long, and you know where they are?" I ask, skeptical of her statement.

"A Catholic Church and hardware stores were my first destinations —yours, on the other hand, were probably not ...."

Seeing I was painting myself into a corner, I relented. "Okay, you win. Seeing you know the locations and our squad car is repaired, you can drive."

"If you don't mind, I'd like to finish my herbal tea first."

I reply, "Sure. I have to contact the Arizona Department of Public Safety and see if they found anything of note at the Madison Building."

Chapter Sixty-Four

As soon as we get into the car, I tell Ruger, "It's your call where we go first."

"If that's the case, then we'll go to Tom's, Mr. Hardware. That's the closest to the station."

"Hey, I'm just a passenger."

She asks, "Before we left, you said you were going to contact Public Safety. What did they come up with?"

"Just as I suspected—nothing."

"These people must be pros," says Ruger as she navigates through the morning traffic. "What they haven't learned on the outside, they get their advanced degree on the inside. And speaking of them, why don't we stake out Two Guns? They are bound to go digging around there, eventually."

"Considering that we only have 24 hours in a day, we both need to sleep, and we'd stand out like a sore thumb because of the open terrain—that's why. Since the murder of Cody Dosela, I've asked the highway patrol to keep an eye out for any unusual activity at Two Guns."

"Actually, that makes sense, but given the distractions they encounter each day, something could get past them."

"Anything's possible," I answer as we approach the hardware store's parking lot.

Ruger says, "Maybe we should try the hardware stores out in Winslow or even as far away as Joseph City?"

"Let's try the ones closest to us first and then work outward."

Ruger exits the highway and eases the car into one of the open angled parking spots.

Before leaving the vehicle, Ruger asks, "Since I'm a steady customer, do you mind if I do all the talking?"

"Fine by me. Since I don't know what a hardware store looks like, maybe I'll meander around the store. Don't forget to grab our photograph and your artist's rendering."

Ruger laughs. "Okay, but whatever you do, I suggest you don't touch anything sharp. You might hurt yourself."

Now, it was my turn to laugh.

Upon entering the store, we split. I head to the brightly colored tool section, remembering Ruger's sarcastic words of caution.

I heard a voice calling out in the background, "Hi, Emily. What can we do for you today?"

The store had narrow canyons of screws, nails, valves, electrical parts, and, of course, tools—all encapsulated in plastic or brightly colored boxes. I was only joking with Ruger about my unfamiliarity with hardware stores. This was not my first rodeo, as the expression goes, but this was the first hardware store I could think of that had everything. It was a throwback to the old Western general store.

I found myself barely in the heart of the store before Ruger calls out, "Detective Owens, can you come back here?"

When I met Ruger, she stood beside a jovial, full-faced man with a mustache and a wide smile. He wore a blue baseball cap, jeans, and a chambray shirt. The name tag on his shirt says "Tom," so I assumed he was the owner.

"Detective Owens, I'd like you to meet Tom Loomis. He's the one I give grief to when I'm not around you."

"That's quite an introduction, Tom," I say, extending my hand. "My sympathies."

He laughs. "Emily, here, is one of my favorite customers. You are likely familiar with her talent as an artist. We share art interests—I in photography and she in painting."

"Tom, pleased to meet you. Incidentally, I only just recently discovered how talented she is."

Tom says, "I know you didn't come here to talk about art. Emily showed me the pictures of those two suspects. Yes, they came in here four days ago. I waited on them myself. They got a digging shovel, a drain spade, a stud finder, a sledgehammer, and a small handsaw. I thought it was a strange combination."

I ask, "Why a drain spade?"

"I'm the one who suggested it because they asked me what's a good shovel for removing dirt from a hole."

"Was that it?" asks Ruger.

"No, because I said, 'The ground's pretty hard. You'll probably need a pickaxe, too.'"

I ask, "So, that was it—the shovels, sledgehammer, stud finder, small handsaw, and pickaxe?"

"Like all the hardware stores here in Flagstaff, we carry ammo. They wanted a box of 9mm. I know now that the couple is up to some mischief, but I never gave it a thought. People in these parts are always going to the desert and target practicing."

I ask, "Did they ever say anything unusual or talk about where they might be living?

"I mentioned, you know, just in conversation, that it was too soon to be planting a garden. They both laughed, and the misses says, 'I'm making a rock garden.' At the time, I thought neither of them looked like the domestic types, especially with her all gussied up and wearing that fancy ring on her right thumb."

Knowing people sometimes forget what they consider unimportant, I ask, "That's it? Anything else?"

"This probably isn't that important, but she called him Max. Also, he had either a German or an Austrian accent. I never consider that odd, because we get people from around the world that visit The Grand Canyon or the Meteor Crater."

Chapter Sixty-Five

While Max Becker eases the Oldsmobile Cutlass off Interstate 40, Valerie Vaughn checks the magazine before sliding it into her Sig Sauer. She says, "Go to that gas station and back into one of those empty bays. Wait, on second thought, take the one on the right."

Max says, "It doesn't look safe. I don't vant to hit somezing or blow e tire."

"I'll get out and guide you when we get closer."

Max follows the rough road, turns left before the abandoned station, and takes a right near the front of the building.

"Now kill the lights and turn around. I'll get out to lead you in."

Valerie rolls down the passenger's side window.

The front beams of the car sweep the area before abruptly going dark, but his taillights glow brightly in the nocturnal Arizona desert. Valerie opens the car door. The dome lights shine intensely for a few seconds before ending their radiance at the slamming of the door.

Standing beside the open window, she says, "Now back up slowly, slowly, slowly—stop!"

Valerie assesses the view and then returns to the car. "We'll keep what little heat we have," she says while rolling up the window. "We

231

have just enough view of the area, yet we're pretty well hidden. Kill the engine."

"Vhy are you so confident zose two guys vill come here today?" asks Max.

"The one who works for the city is always off on weekends. So, unless he decides to take off during the week, which is unlikely, that makes the weekends the most likely time for him."

"And zee hotel clerk?"

"I didn't mention this before. I called the hotel and inquired about his off day. The young girl I talked with was rather stupid, so it was easy to get information from her. I said I was an old friend and wanted to stop in to surprise him. She told me he was off today but would be working tomorrow evening. So, it was an easy guess when they planned on looking for the treasure."

Max says, "I takin zee nap."

"Go ahead. It's early. It's a little past five."

Valerie adjusts her seat to where she feels comfortable and, at the same time, positioned to observe the comings and goings of Interstate 40's traffic.

After nearly an hour of fighting nodding off, she says, "Max, get up. It's starting to get light out."

"Vat time is it?"

Valerie checks her watch. "Ten to seven."

"Vat ve do now?" says Max, then yawns.

"We wait," she replies, then adds, "Hold on, hold on. I think our treasure hunters are coming in now." Valerie stiffens and then leans forward on the dash. Her eyes follow the yellow AMC Pacer as it passes the gas station. "Now we wait and let them do all the work."

"Vey ve buy all ze tools?" asks Max.

"Just in case, Max, just in case."

Chapter Sixty-Six

"Are you sure we can dig into this stuff?" asks Doug. He kicks at the hard topsoil with his boot. "It's like cement."

"No problemo, my main man," says Ralph, holding the metal detector over the site that just proved the most promising to their search. "We'll take turns with the pickaxe. I'll chop, then you chop."

Doug says, "I guess we have no choice but to dig. The map says this is the spot, and the metal detector confirms it when it went crazy over the location."

Ralph points to the terminus of the road at his feet, where the debris from the old Route 66 ends. "Hey man, check this out. Someone in the road crew working on the new highway starts digging up the old road and spots an unusual-looking box. A treasure chest, he thinks, but he stays cool because he wants to hog it for himself—whatever it is. He plans on coming back, but something happens."

"Like what?" asks Doug.

"Dunno. Maybe he's kickin' the bucket, and his dying words are about the treasure?"

"Like who?"

"The dude that got offed in your hotel. You know, like in the movie, *It's a Mad, Mad, Mad, Mad, World*."

"Ralph, you've been watching too many movies."

"Maybe I'm right-on."

"Ralph, I think we should be doing more digging than figgerin'."

"Okay, man, I'll go first, and you do the dirt hauling."

Ralph tests the ground with a few taps of his pickaxe before raising it over his shoulder, then lets loose. "Cowabunga!" he yells as the tool strikes the ground. The tip of the pickaxe barely makes a dimple in the soil, but its impact sends tiny fragments flying in all directions. "Bummer," he grumbles. Undaunted, he resumes his stance and begins pummeling the area while Doug backs away from the shower of dirt.

Ralph continues his relentless pounding for nearly half an hour before saying, "It's your turn, Bud," and hands the pickaxe to Doug. "So, what are we going to find, a big Wells Fargo strongbox?"

"Once I found out about this treasure, I did some research. The gold and silver are hidden in two five-gallon whiskey kegs."

"Why did they do that?" asks Ralph, wiping his brow with the sleeve of his coat.

"To hide the fact it's a gold and silver shipment."

"Okay, man, but say these guys do the heist and see two five-gallon barrels of whiskey. Now, if it was me, I'd steal the hootch. Maybe they should have marked the stuff flour or sugar?"

"Good point, Ralph, but they figured it was an inside job anyway, and it wouldn't have mattered."

"I don't know, man. They must have been pretty stupid back then. Here, your turn." Ralph hands Doug the pickaxe.

After Doug takes his turn, he says with satisfaction, "We're making progress. Let's use the crowbar to pry loose some of this old roadbed." Happily, Ralph goes to the trunk and secures the bar and metal detector. Returning to the dig site, he says, "Let's check if we're getting closer." He turns on the machine, and it emits a series of beeps. He places it over the widening hole, and the beeping sound becomes a shriek.

"I'm having a good feeling about this, Ralph. What's your guess before we hit pay dirt?"

"We still got a lotta stuff to clear away, man. Maybe, ah, maybe another couple of hours."

Chapter Sixty-Seven

S tanding outside Tom's, Mr. Hardware store, I remark, "I gotta hunch this might be a good day for us to take a trip to Two Guns."

"Why this particular day?" asks Ruger.

"For one thing, I don't doubt for a minute that dame with the fancy ring wants to get that treasure in Two Guns as soon as possible and get the hell out of Flagstaff."

I start moving towards our car, and Ruger follows. I take the driver's side, and she opens the passenger side door.

"Had enough of my driving already?" says Ruger.

"Oh, I guess it was force of habit. You wanna drive?" I ask.

"Nah, you take the reins, I'll enjoy the scenery."

Once inside, I turn the ignition key.

Ruger says, "Now, let's assume the same people did the million-plus dollars take from the Madeison Building. Don't you think that would be enough of a haul?"

"In my book, there are two things that are common among criminals. First, they are dumb. Second, they are greedy. Right now, I'm not sure how all this stuff went down. Did they come here mostly for the Wells Fargo robbery, or did they come here for the cash hidden in the

Madison building? It's the age-old story of the chicken or the egg—what came first?"

Ruger says, "The fact that Sam Jackson, aka, Oscar Eugene Burrows, was killed in the first place tells me it was a double cross."

I nod. "And Paul Grendon's death was a triple cross."

Ruger laughs. "I'm not sure if it's a triple cross. Technically, I think it's still a double cross, but I'm not going to split hairs."

I put the car in gear and start backing out.

I ask, "Are you hungry?"

"Yep, sort of. What I had this morning really wasn't enough."

"Mr. Bob's is on the way. How about a brunch there?"

"Well," Ruger answers, "It has my kind of food. Why not?"

"Mr. Bob's it is," I say and push down on the accelerator.

From the corner of my eye, I see Ruger studying me. "Something bothering you?" I ask.

"I was just thinking. Suddenly, out of the clear blue, you think it's a good day to go to Two Guns. I think you're not telling me everything."

I smile and say, "You are turning out to be quite a detective."

"So, there is more to this outing?"

"Yeah. The part about Valerie Vaughn wantin' to get her hands on the gold and silver is pure speculation on my part, but logical. She's a greedy person—pure and simple."

"It's not only that," she scoffs, "It's those two young guys, that McGuire and his pal Ralph, right?"

"You got me. After I called the lab people, I called the Double Six Hotel and asked to speak with McGuire. I knew he works the graveyard shift, but I only wanted to see what he was up to. That girl, ah ... Phyllis Logan, really can't keep a secret or understand personal privacy. Luckily for me, though, she told me he was off today and probably was with his pal Ralph."

"That may be, but she was talking to you—a cop. I think anyone would have done the same."

I shrugged. "Perhaps."

"Shouldn't we have gone to Two Guns after visiting the hardware store?"

"I have to admit," I began, "this whole situation about buried treasure really intrigued me. My first source of information was from Kowalski. Local history is his hobby. He told me many things about the area and people's interest in buried treasure. I also was interested in its geology. I found out that digging for buried treasure is difficult because, in some areas, it's like digging into cement."

"So, you think time is on our side?" asks Ruger.

I reply, "Now that we know what everyone is after and its relative location, whoever starts to dig it isn't going to be easy."

Ruger says, "Okay, I understand, but if we are following the trail of outlaws who buried treasure, didn't they have a hard time burying their loot?"

"That's precisely my reasoning, too. This is what I think happened. The gold and silver were heavy. So, as they started for their hideout, they found a depression in the ground. Taking advantage of the situation, they dumped the stolen gold and silver into a ready-made spot."

Ruger laughs. "They just happened to find a hole in the ground?"

"Think about it. They are on the run and panic. The hole was there, and all they had to do was throw the stuff in the hole and cover it up with the surrounding dirt and rock."

"Where did you get all this information?" asks Ruger.

"Most of it, like I mentioned, I got from Kowalski. He's the one who figured the haul was too heavy to travel with the robbers, so they buried it along the way. After the shootout at Veit Springs, the local authorities and Veit, who later bought the land solely for excavating for its presumed burial spot of the stagecoach robbery's loot, never found a single piece of gold."

Ruger snorts, "Then it becomes a mystery and legend."

"Yep, you are right," I agree. "Then, probably, in this case, it gets inadvertently buried under Route 66. Later, it gets accidentally discovered when they reroute Route 66 into Highway 40."

"And the person who found it had every intention to return, but for some reason, he doesn't."

"Uh-uh, which brings us to today and Mr. Bob's."

Chapter Sixty-Eight

"We gotta be getting close," says Ralph. "We've been at this for six hours. I don't know about you, man, but I'm getting bushed."

"Gimmy that pickaxe, Ralph. I'll take over for a while."

Ralph walks over to where Doug sits in the opened driver's side doorway of the Pacer. "No problem, man. Here."

Doug takes the pickaxe, retraces Ralph's footpath, and, with forceful blows, begins hammering into the debris. His work is almost manic, pounding and pounding without losing a beat. Then, when the tip of the pick mattock hits something with a dull thud, Doug abruptly stops.

"Hey, Ralph, get over here! I think I hit pay-dirt."

Doug notices how Ralph, obviously tired by the way he slowly rolls off the Pacer's seat, makes a determined effort toward him.

Doug dances in place. "Ralph, I think we finally found the gold! We found it! We found it!"

Ralph's enthusiasm begins to percolate as well. Seized by Doug's gusto, he shouts, "Bitchin'! We're gonna be rich!"

"C'mon, Ralph, help me clear away this stuff."

The two men feverishly pick and shovel, and at times, get in each other's way until the opening is wide enough to haul out the desiccated kegs.

"Holy cow," shouts Doug as they bring the treasure to the surface. "We've actually found it."

"Excellent, my main man, excellent," says Ralph as he does an impromptu jig, circling the area in wild abandonment.

Doug looks up and spots a car approaching along the frontage road that borders the interstate. "Ralph, a car's coming."

Ralph, still in his euphoric state, continues his dance unabated.

"Ralph! A car is heading our way. Get your shotgun."

"Uh?"

"A car, Ralph—a car. It's coming this way. Hurry, get your gun," shouts Doug.

Ralph comes out of his frolicking, pauses, and then dashes for the Pacer's open trunk. As he reached for the shotgun, a tuff of dirt explodes in front of him. With the gun now in his hand, he pumps a round into the chamber and blindly aims toward the oncoming car. He pulls the trigger, and nothing happens. Realizing he didn't fully engage the round, he ejects it and pumps another into the chamber, then pulls the trigger. It explodes toward the advancing car. It stops.

Doug, his body pressed hard against the ground, unbuttons his coat enough to grab his revolver. Using the berm as cover that was created by previous digging by crews, who worked to plow under remnants of Route 66, fires one shot at the Oldsmobile Cutlass. The reaction is immediate as two returning rounds zing over Doug's head, then explode on the top of the ridge.

"Ralph! Get over here."

Hunched over and using part of the vehicle as a shield, Ralph makes a dash for Doug's position behind the berm.

Two more muffled rounds hit close to Ralph's feet as he dives over the embankment.

"You okay?"

"Not sure," says Ralph as he rubs his legs.

Doug examines him and says, "I don't see any blood."

Ralph, his voice tense, says, "Man, this is mega serious."

"I think I got range on them with my .22," says Doug, "but they got us outgunned."

Ralph, lying on his back, says, "Holy ambush, Batman. I think we got us a Mexican standoff."

Chapter Sixty-Nine

"That was another terrific meal," says Ruger as we make our way onto Interstate 40. "Too bad it isn't closer to the station."

I answer, "It's funny, we both like Mr. Bob's, but for completely different reasons."

Ruger laughs. "Maybe the United Nations should have lunch there?"

"Yeah, sure," I reply with a laugh.

Like the last time we ate there, I was content sitting back and enjoying the afterglow of a great meal in silence. Ruger must also have felt the same way because she, too, sat there quietly, looking out at the passing desert.

It wasn't until we passed Winona that she broke her meditation. "Did you ever have time to go to the Meteor Crater? It's a little past Two Guns."

"I've heard of it. You've been there?"

Ruger nods, and says, "It's really a neat spot."

"It's just a big hole in the ground, right?"

"Well," she replies indignantly, "so is the Grand Canyon if you look at it through cynical eyes."

"I'm sure it's a nice hole, as holes go, but that doesn't turn me on." After I said that, I hoped she would let the matter drop.

"You're missing the point," she says dryly. "It's the experience of standing at the edge and thinking what it was like 50,000 years ago."

Okay, I thought, do you really want to continue this argument? "I wasn't around 50,000 years ago, so it's hard to imagine."

"You know what you lack?" she hisses.

"Deodorant?

After a derisive laugh, she says, "Culture."

At that point, I surmised the discussion was over.

As we turn left over the Canyon Padre Bridge, the traffic crawls to a stop.

Ruger says, "It looks bad. It looks like there's also a fire."

"Yeah," I agree and pump the brakes.

Ruger cranes her neck over the dashboard. "Well, the flashing lights tell me the highway patrol guys are on site."

I say, "It looks like they are rerouting traffic off the 225 exit. I'll turn on the CB and see what the truckers are saying."

Ruger asks, "We gonna budge the line?"

"We'll see how fast the traffic flow goes. We seem to be moving along okay. I hate to cause more of a problem than need be."

"Yeah," says Ruger, "It gives us more time to spend together."

Now, it was my time to laugh.

Chapter Seventy

Doug and Ralph both lie face down, with little ground cover to protect them—precariously hold their position.

Ralph says, "Doug, we can't stay like this forever. How much ammo you got?"

"Nine, I mean eight now. I got a partial box in the glove compartment. How many you got?"

"Three in my howitzer. Maybe I got nineteen keeping company in the trunk of your car."

"I don't like the odds, Ralph."

"Hey, man, this is just like Butch Cassidy and the Sundance Kid shootout."

"Yeah," Doug answers. "Just like. Do you remember how that movie ended?"

"Badly, man, badly."

"Ralph, it's gonna get dark in maybe three hours."

"So, what are you sayin', man?"

"I'm saying, when it does, they're gonna rush us, and we won't stand a chance with our limited firepower. We gotta get that ammo before that happens."

"Doug, I made it once already. If you could cover me with your gun, that should give me enough of an edge."

"It sounds okay, but once I offload my eight rounds," says Doug, "you'll havta be back here with all the ammo."

"I can do it, man. James Bond did it in *The Man with the Golden Gun*. Bond only had a six-shot magazine, and he brought down Scaramanga."

"Ralph, that was the movie. This is real life!"

"When I go over the top, you start pumping out rounds."

"Ralph, you are batshit crazy."

"The only casualty may be your wheels, man. It will be a bit sticky when I reach into the trunk."

"I don't care about my car, Ralph. I don't want to see you dead. Got that?"

"Have no fear, I'm here," boasts Ralph.

Doug points toward the Oldsmobile Cutlass. "They're coming closer. Shit, we gotta go for it now, Ralph."

"Okay, man. Remember when we practiced, shoot high for range."

"Yeah, yeah. You better get going, Ralph."

Without another word, Ralph dashes toward the car. He hears Doug's gun fire twice. He opens the driver's side of the Pacer's door and crawls on his stomach to reach the glove compartment. As he opens it, one shot finds its mark somewhere on the engine block, and two smash the windshield. A shower of safety glass fragments falls on him. Shoving the box of .22 rounds into his pocket, he inches his way out.

One more shot rings out from Doug's revolver.

Ralph mumbles under his breath, "Five more shots, Doug. Five more shots."

Doug's hand shakes as he aims, waiting for Ralph to make his final move.

Ralph takes several breaths and then lunges toward the side of the trunk. As he peers around the edge of the car, a volley of rounds kick up dirt near him. The frightful thumping of bullets peppering the Pacer's shell makes Ralph's stomach queasy.

"What are you waiting for?" Ralph loudly chastises Doug.

"Oh, yeah ... for my return trip."

Ralph carefully eyes the open trunk and spots the box of shotgun shells. "It's now or never," he says to himself, gathering courage for the last leap.

Doug fires two shots at the advancing car. It stops and wonders if he got lucky.

Ralph continues the conversation to himself. "Three shots left. Man, only three shots left. Shit, I'm gonna be toast. Here goes nothing," he yells, diving for the box of ammo.

Chapter Seventy-One

Over the hiss of the CB comes a report that unnerved me.
"Something funny is going on over at that Two Guns spot. Over," says the trucker known only as Shadow Man.

"Ten-four," another responds. "Yep, I saw that as I was heading west toward Flagstaff. Over."

Shadow Man says, "I swear it looks like a gunfight."

"Ten-four, Shadow Man. Breaker, breaker, stay clear of Two Guns."

I turn down the volume. Ruger's eyes meet mine.

"Time for the light show?" asks Ruger.

"Turn 'em on," I say while activating the siren.

I break free from the line of cars and move doggedly along its periphery. Because of the narrow shoulder, I was more concerned about some overly eager driver moving into my path.

Ruger says, "Some of these people are either deaf or just plain stupid."

I answer, "Right now, I'm worried about the stupid ones who decide to cut in front of me.

Even with the wail of the siren, our movement is governed by the narrowness of the shoulder on the off-ramp.

Ruger says, "Whatever's going on at Two Guns, I don't think we can get any help from the Highway Patrol guys."

"You're right. My guess is that our boys, Doug McGuire and Ralph Tyler, have got themselves into a hornet's nest."

"Can't we move any faster?" Ruger asks, pulling her .38 Special from its holster.

"First time?" I ask.

"Uh-huh," she says with hesitation. "And you ... how many?"

"More than I care to. Remember, I came here to get away from the mean streets of New York City."

Ruger clumsily opens the cylinder of her revolver.

I didn't want Ruger to choke under fire. I say, "Calm down. They're not expecting us—we'll have the element of surprise. Do you carry a speed loader?"

"Un-huh. On the range, I could reload in 6 seconds."

I say, "When I was a rookie, I remember doing as well, but as you know, reloading under fire has its own issues."

"You said we'll have the element of surprise. How do you figure that? After all, we're coming in hot with lights and sirens blazing."

"About two miles out of Two Guns, we'll run silent. We're in an unmarked vehicle, which will give us some cover. I remember seeing McGuire's yellow AMC Pacer. If he's using that car, it will be easy to spot. The rest will be up to pure luck."

Ruger says, "And if not ... I mean the part of the yellow Pacer?"

"According to Cassie, the waitress, our mystery lady with the fancy ring, is driving a maroon Oldsmobile Cutlass. I doubt they have any reason to change wheels at this point."

As we clear the logjam at the cloverleaf interchange, I press hard on the accelerator and rocket past traffic. "Had I known we would be in a standoff, I would have requested a rifle. My .38 Colt Special will have to do." I place it on the car seat next to me.

"What kinda range do you have on that?" asks Ruger.

"With its five-inch barrel, I could get lucky at 100 yards."

Ruger asks, "You don't know what they have."

"Yes, we do," I counter. "They have a 9mm, based on what ammo they bought at the hardware store."

"And the range of that?" asks Ruger.

"Effectively, 50 yards. Luckily, maybe 100 yards. Considering the bullet pattern of Jackson's death, I'd say she's an expert, and I would lean to the 20-yard estimate."

Chapter Seventy-Two

As Ralph dives into the trunk of the Pacer, more shots rip through the car's body. He finds the repetitive plunk, plunk, plunk of phantom bullets unnerving. With labored breathing, he contemplates his exit after wedging himself into a fetal position. Now, he found himself between two options: stay or run. Either way, the danger of getting hit was real.

Doug calls out. "Ralph! You okay?"

"Yeah."

"C'mon back—I'm running out of ammo."

"Hold your horses, man. I'll get there," answers Ralph as he twists his way to get more of an advantage when he springs out. The car rocks back and forth.

More rounds—plunk, plunk, plunk, plunk.

He wasn't counting but just thought about Clint Eastwood and, "You've got to ask yourself one question. 'Do I feel lucky?' Well, do ya, punk" *It was a gamble. Did they reload, or aren't they counting?*

"Ralph!" Doug shouts. "Are you coming?"

"Here I come, pal ... lay down that suppressor fire." Ralph says before rolling out of the trunk and dashing toward the berm.

Although egged on by Doug's own words, Ralph's hasty retreat appeared to have caught Doug off guard. As a result, Doug fired only one round at the approaching Oldsmobile Cutlass. Luckily, only one round was countered in return. Doug wondered if it was intentional or if they had run out of ammunition. It was the same time Ralph dived over the crest of accumulated gravel.

That one shot proved deadly enough. Ralph yells, "I'm hit!"

"Hang on, Ralph, hang on. Gimme the bullets, they're closing in on us."

Wincing in pain, Ralph tosses the box of .22 rounds to Doug and lies back, groaning.

Doug's hands shake uncontrollably. He flips open the cylinder of his revolver and ejects all spent casings, including the one unfired round. With the ammo box close by his side, he begins to chamber each round. His shaking hands making it difficult for him to reload.

"I think I'm dying," moans Ralph.

Doug closes the cylinder and immediately fires blindly at the Oldsmobile Cutlass. It stops and retreats.

Doug shouts, "Go back, you bastards!" He then turns to check on Ralph.

"I think I'm really hit bad, pal," Ralph whines.

"Lemme see," says Doug while pulling up the right pants leg of Ralph's blue genes. "Yep. You definitely got hurt, Ralph, but I don't think that cut came from a bullet. It appears to be a scrape from road debris. Now get up. We gotta get ready. I think they're gonna make another attempt to rush us."

Ralph looks at his slightly bloodied leg, then straightens his Levi's.

Doug returns to his post and reloads.

Taking up the position beside Doug, Ralph inserts five shells into his shotgun.

"I think this will be their final attack," says Doug.

Ralph says, "This is how John Wayne died in the Alamo."

"You mean Davy Crockett, don't you?" answers Doug.

"I'm talking about the movie, man."

"Here they come, Ralph. We gotta make sure our return fire counts. Wait until they get closer before firing."

Ralph cries, "'Remember the Alamo!'"

Chapter Seventy-Three

"There they are!" shouts Ruger as we approach Two Guns.

"Yep, I see them. Looks pretty quiet."

Ruger says, "It's probably a standoff."

"Not now, I don't think," I reply. "It looks like they are going in for the kill. I rolled down all our windows. "I'm gonna take it nice and slow unless all hell breaks loose. When I start down the off-ramp, keep an eye on the Cutlass, especially the passenger side's occupant."

"I know the highway patrol people are busy," says Ruger, "but don't you think we should at least let them know what's going down?"

"Yeah, call it in, but we won't wait for the cavalry to arrive."

"All units, all units, officer needs assistance …," Ruger begins her call for help. As we exit the offramp and pass the Cutlass, she notes the occupants and includes their descriptions in her broadcast.

"The woman on the passenger side gave me a look of recognition like she knows we're cops," says Ruger.

"We'll see if they bolt when we come up behind," I reply before making a hard right down the frontage road.

"Owens, do you hear the popping racket from the yellow Pacer? They are definitely engaged in a firefight."

"Okay, Ruger, we're going in hot. Hit the lights."

With emergency lights flashing and siren blaring, I stomp on the gas pedal. Moving within a fifty yards of the Cutlass, the occupant on the passenger side opens fire. The round hits dead center on our windshield. The medium-sized hole forms a spider fracture that spreads.

I yell, "Let 'em have it!"

Ruger leans out of the opening, yet still constrained by her seatbelt, and fires four quick shots at the fleeing vehicle.

The Cutlass abandons the side road and quickly turns left down the gravel road. With its wheels spinning, a cloud of dirt billows behind it as it speeds up. I, too, twirl left but choose the angled road instead, hoping to intersect their path.

"It appears they're going for the Diablo Bridge," says Ruger. "We're closing on them. Should I open fire?"

My mind is racing as we get closer. "Did you reload?"

"Yeah," she says, her right arm at the ready.

"The woman's on the passenger side. If she shoots, she'll have to do it in front of the driver. I don't think that's likely."

"I'm ready," says Ruger.

I answer, "Take your shot when we come to the intersection. We can't let them cross the bridge. If they do, it'll be harder to catch them in that open country."

"Any time," Ruger says, her arm now extended past the opening, gripping her gun with both hands.

"Now!" I shout.

In rapid succession, she empties her revolver. The car, nearing the bridge, fishtails. I see it skid, then appear to lose control before careening off its right side. For a second, it's airborne as it plunges into the canyon. Having gained momentum during the chase, I hit the brakes and screech to a halt.

Without a word, Ruger and I open our doors and run to the canyon's edge. Looking down, I see movement from the right side of the vehicle. The door opens, and a woman rolls out onto the rocks below. As she lies there, writhing in pain, the smoke billows from the engine compartment and then bursts into flame. The woman rolls further away.

"Ruger, call it in. I'm going down to see what I can do."
The car explodes.

Chapter Seventy-Four

As I make my way down to the burning car, I think about all the situations I have encountered during my career. My descent down a canyon to rescue a woman near a burning vehicle was to be my first. Fortunately for me, she had rolled far enough away from the flames. Despite that, the heat radiated enough for me to consider the reality of the danger. Halfway down, I realized the trip up wouldn't be as easy.

Now, within talking distance, I see she has rested herself onto her side, with her back to me. I pull out my revolver and call out to her, "You are under arrest. Do not attempt to resist."

She moans. She raises her right arm. As her hand becomes visible, I see the distinctive ring and a gun.

"Drop it," I yell. "If you don't, I'll be forced to shoot. I mean it. Drop it!"

I sense some hesitation in her. Her hand loosens before the gun drops.

From inside the burning Cutlass, a series of sharp exploding rounds of ammo cooking off unnerved me as I drew closer. With her body still blocking her abandoned weapon, I approached her cautiously until I saw it lying by her side.

Advancing from the rear, I say, "Do not move. Where are you hurting?"

"My leg. I think I'm shot in my leg."

"Hang on. I'm going to pull you back."

"My leg! It hurts."

Realizing the urgency of moving away from the flames, I ignored her plea. I turned her over onto her back and began pulling her away from the danger. Once we were at a safe distance, I tended to her wounds. She had indeed been hit by one of Ruger's bullets. Although her injury wasn't life-threatening, it required attention. I remove my tie. Using it as a tourniquet, I stemmed the flow of blood.

Ruger yells down to me. "I called it in. Help is on the way."

The shade from the opposite side of the canyon gradually creeps its way toward us. Once in its shadow, I knew the temperature would drop. There wasn't a doubt in my mind that I was looking at the elusive Valerie Vaughn—the ruthless killer. Yet her present incapacity made her appear frail. Seeing she was in shock and shaking, I removed my coat and, using it as a blanket, covered her.

She smiled at me weakly.

Chapter Seventy-Five

"**M**an! Did you see that?" yells Ralph.

"Yeah," Doug replies with a deep sigh of relief. "Let's see if my car works after all that shooting."

Both men brush themselves off and go back to the dig. Doug says, "There it is, Ralph, our future. Let's load it into the trunk before seeing what happened at the bridge."

"I don't know, man. Maybe we should boogie outta here? I don't want to talk to the man."

"Listen, Ralph. We have done nothing wrong. The police know who we are. We searched for the treasure that hundreds of people have been looking for over the years. We found it fair and square. No. We'll pack it up, go over to the bridge, and see what's happenin'."

"I guess you're right, man."

After clearing each of the wooden kegs from the hole, they both carried them, one by one, to the car.

"We're not going to fit our treasure and the equipment into the trunk," says Doug. "Let's shove the metal detector and digging tools in the back seat."

"Yeah, the sooner we skip, the sooner we par-tee."

Having secured their gear, Doug checks the engine while Ralph inspects the tires. They get into their car, and Doug turns over the engine. "It works!" he yells.

"Can you see good enough through the windshield?" asks Ralph.

As they pull away from the treasure site, Doug says, "They got one of our headlights."

"You can still see, okay?" asks Ralph.

"Yeah, yeah. It's just a slow go, that's all."

A patrol car, a fire department truck with its water tanker truck, a Coconino County Search & Rescue vehicle, and an ambulance exit the freeway and speed past, sirens and lights broadcasting their arrival.

Doug says, "When we get there, be cool, Ralph. Don't say anything about the treasure. Remember, we weren't breaking the law—we were shooting back in self-defense. Got that?"

"My lips are sealed, good buddy. What are you gonna say to the man?"

"Frankly, I'm nervous. I'll play it by ear."

"Hey, man. Maybe they're gonna start shooting at us?"

"What for?"

"Hey, they did that in *Bonnie and Clyde,*" says Ralph, craning his neck nervously forward as they approach the collection of emergency vehicles.

"Ralph, you are the only person I know who leads a double life. Just be cool and shut up. Let me do the talking."

They roll to a stop, and Doug shuts off the engine and kills the light.

Both Doug and Ralph exit the car. A nearby uniformed officer shouts, "Get back in your car. This is a crime scene."

They hesitate before Detective Ruger says, "It's all right, officer. We will want them for questioning."

Detective Ruger motions for them to come closer. She points. "You two, sit over there until I can have time to talk with you."

Doug and Ralph move in the general direction she pointed, but pick a spot closer to the canyon's rim. They watch as rescuers lower a Stokes litter down the rocky embankment. Several calls go back and forth among the rescuers. Among the participants, someone shouts," Rocks!" What follows is a frantic collection of orders from both levels. Finally, an order is given, "Pull 'er up."

Both Doug and Ralph watch as the injured party is loaded into the ambulance before being sprinted away. The two detectives they know, Detective Owens and Detective Ruger, converse with the other emergency personnel before being dismissed, leaving the fire department to do their job of dousing the flames. Finished, they both converge on them.

"So, gentlemen, you just couldn't stay away," says Detective Owens.

"We didn't do anything wrong," declares Doug.

"Whatcha got in that car that's full of holes?" asks Detective Ruger.

"Something we found," answers Doug.

"Let's have a look-see," says Owens.

The sun dropped below the horizon, leaving only the early remains of dusk. With flashlights in hand, both detectives use them to guide their way toward the car.

"You wanna pop that trunk?" asks Detective Owens.

Doug removes the car keys from his pocket and unlocks the trunk. There, weathered by years of abandonment, two wood casks highlighted under the trunk's light.

"Well, well, now what is that?" asks Detective Ruger.

"It's our treasure," answers Ralph. "We found it, 'finder's keepers, loser's weepers.'"

Doug drops his head and shakes it back and forth.

"Did you know that just last year, the Federal Government passed the Archaeological Resources Protection Act, making removing treasure from certain lands illegal?"

"Huh?" says Ralph.

"Listen, I don't care one way or other," says Detective Owens. "It's late, we have to do a report, and you two will need to report to my office tomorrow. No excuses. Got that?"

"Yeah," says Doug.

"And a word of caution," says Detective Ruger. "You probably have a small fortune in that trunk of yours. I would take special care that it doesn't become a magnet for criminals—if you know what I mean?"

Doug remarks, "Like, only we know about what we found. Who else knows about it?"

Detective Owens begins, "Okay, we are going to return to the station and fill out our report. This news will likely reach the local newspapers and possibly the national press. You two will become celebrities overnight. Believe me, you will not like the attention."

"We gotta go, " says Detective Ruger. "Oh, and by the way, you need to fix your headlight. I don't want to give you a ticket."

"What are we gonna do?" asks Doug. "I gotta work tomorrow, and so do you. I'm already on thin ice."

"Work? We don't haveta work, Buddy," says Ralph. "We're rich!"

They leave the smothering wreckage behind them and get in the yellow AMC Pacer. Both smile at their good fortune as they slowly drive away.

Chapter Seventy-Six

Doug McGuire and Ralph Tyler sat before me in the interrogation room, blurry-eyed and fidgeting. I ask, "Did either of you two read the morning paper this morning?"

Both men shake their heads.

The morning paper sat unopened on my side of the table, with the front page facing down. I took it, flipped it over to the above-the-fold section, then slammed it down, face up.

Their eyes widened.

"Before I cut you loose to the wolves, I want to know what happened prior to our arrival at Two Guns?"

They remained silent.

"Now listen up. You two are aren't in trouble with the law, but you will be if you continue to withhold information related to this case. Do you understand?"

They sheepishly nod.

Doug McGuire spoke up. "Ralph here borrowed the metal detector from work, and I took a day off to hunt for the treasure. We felt it was a sure thing, guided by the map and the detector. And it turned out to be just that, a sure thing."

"When did they start shooting at you?"

"They must have been watching us for a long time. It wasn't until we hit the jackpot that they decided to move in."

I ask, "We're either of you wounded?"

"Yeah, man. I took a hit to the leg," says Ralph.

"Why didn't you say something when the ambulance was there?"

"No one asked us if we were hurt," says Doug. "Detective, it's past and no longer an issue. Ralph is playing the drama queen. He got a scratch from jumping into our position. That's all it is."

Ralph snaps, "Well, it still was an injury."

With my patience wearing thin, I say, "Listen, you two, I have to get going. You both are on notice that you will be required to testify at the trial of Valerie Vaughn. Do you understand?"

Both nod.

The door opens, and Detective Ruger steps in. She says, "Hey, McGuire and Tyler, you got quite a mob of reporters waiting for you out front. Seems they want more information about the *treasure hunters*. Detective Owens, if you're done, I can let them out the back door."

I ask, "What will it be, the fame and glory or the run for cover?"

Ralph laughs without consulting with his pal and says, "We'll go for the fame and glory."

I shake my head in puzzlement and say, "Detective Ruger, send them to the wolves."

* * *

Ruger and I got into our replacement vehicle with the admonishment from the motor pool chief, "Try to avoid the bullets on this one."

Yeah, I thought, *we'll be the joke of the department for at least a week.*

I ask Ruger, "How did you happen to come by your information about that Resources Protection Act?"

"Unlike your unique attachment to scotch and baking, my interests vary from art, astronomy, and archeology. In short, I strive to stay informed about the news. In all honesty, the only reason I remembered that act was because it had been passed just last year in 1979."

"Ruger, I always thought I was a smartass, but you beat me in spades."

She says, "I consider that a compliment."

To which I reply, "Which it was meant to be,"

Again, there was that moment of silence.

She clears her throat. "Oh, I forgot to mention my conversation with the fire department."

"Oh?" I ask.

"That million-plus dollars taken from the Madison went up in smoke. What little survived amounted to a few small pieces of charred bills."

I reply, "So, they planned on making another score before leaving the area. When you think about it, it was almost the perfect crime and an excuse to kill for it."

"Yep," Ruger replies, "until two dunderheads got involved."

I answer, "I think there may be more to this story after we talk with Valerie Vaughn."

Chapter Seventy-Seven

Like all hospitals, the Flagstaff Medical Center smelled of disinfectant with a hint of misery. A uniformed officer was sitting outside the entrance to Valerie Vaughn's room. He must have been a rookie, because neither Ruger nor I recognized him. We produced our badges and went in.

Vaughn was sitting upright and watching television. My impression was that she was enjoying a pain-free respite.

She looks at me and says, "Thanks for saving my life."

I don't reply.

We come closer to her bedside. I remove the TV controller from her handcuffed arm, turn it off, and set it aside—out of her reach. "Ms. Vaughn, you have been given your right to remain silent. Anything you say to us is not off the record. Do you understand?"

"Yeah. Get on with it. You're interfering with my soaps."

Ruger pulls out her notepad.

I ask, "Do you admit to the killing of Samuel Jackson, aka Oscar Eugene Burrows?"

She laughs. "Do you really expect me to confess to a murder I haven't committed?"

"Okay. Do you admit to the killing of Paul Grendon?"

Now reacting more soberly, she says, "I don't know who you are talking about."

Undeterred, I continue. "Our records show you visited Mr. Grendon several years ago while he was imprisoned in Nevada at the Stewart Conservation Camp."

"It must be someone else," she snaps back.

"Did you know that Mr. Grendon was a former employee of the CIA?"

Like Peter denying Jesus, she scoffs, "I told you, I don't know him."

"That man who died in that fire at Two Guns, who was he?"

"I'm glad you ask. I met him in Winslow. We had lunch together."

"What was his name?"

"Max, ah, Max ... Bäcker. Yeah, you know, I wonder if he didn't kill those two guys?"

"Don't play dumb with us, sister. We have your signature on the prison's logbooks, and you appear on the Double Six's security system."

"You got nothing on me—otherwise, you wouldn't be here."

I reply, "No, I came here to offer you some leniency and avoid a trip to Death Row in Florence."

She says, "Well, Detective, you wasted your time. Gimme my TV control back and get out of here."

I hand her the device. "Confess and live—your choice."

She turns on the remote.

* * *

Ruger was the first to talk on our way back to the station. "Do you think she'll be able to beat the rap?"

"I don't think so, but with the right judge and jury, anything's possible. They call it plausible deniability."

"What's our next stop?" asks Ruger.

"You wrote down the name of that Max guy, didn't you?

Ruger pulls out her notebook. "Max Becker or Max Bäcker. I'm not sure of the spelling."

I reply, "That's interesting."

"How so?" asks Ruger.

"Don't you think that a German boyfriend is a little odd?"

"Hey, it happens," retorts Ruger.

"I have a hunch. Let's go back to the station and visit the evidence room."

Ruger asks, "Why?"

"Something we may have overlooked."

Chapter Seventy-Eight

R uger unlocks the cage to the evidence room and asks, "What are we looking for?"

"I want to examine Valerie Vaughn's personal effects."

We both put on latex gloves.

Ruger goes to one of the file cabinets and fingers through several folders. "Here are her items. The guns and other stuff are kept on another shelf."

Ruger hands the bag to me, and I go to the nearby table to empty the contents onto it. I grab the ring.

"Hmm," I muse.

"What's so special about the ring?" asks Ruger.

"If I think what I think it is, we have a connection between Valerie Vaughn and Max Bäcker. I want to sign this out and take it to The Barn Guys."

"Okay," she relents and slips it into another pouch. "You got my curiosity."

* * *

The Barn Guys' shop was busier than on my last visit. I noticed Chet talking with a customer or a friend, and Rick was finishing a sale at the front counter.

Chet glances at us while Rick shoots us a hiya nod. Not wanting to interfere, Ruger and I mill about and peruse the merchandise. The customer at the counter leaves, and Rick joins us.

"What can I help the Flagstaff Police Department with today?" he asks.

I took the envelope with the ring out of my jacket pocket and handed it to him.

"Whoa! I have only seen this ring once before," says Rick. "They're worth a lot of money."

"That woman who bought those crutches was wearing this ring."

Rick shrugs. "As I remember, she was quite a looker. Maybe I didn't notice her ring."

I ask, "Do you know its history?"

"You bet I do. That lightning bolt isn't an ordinary lightning bolt." Rick points to the center design. "That represented an SA, German for Storm Division or Storm Trooper. The so-called lightning is in the shape of an SA. That organization predated the SS, known as the *Schutzstaffel*. Is there anything else you need to know?"

"No," I said. "You have been very helpful. Thanks again."

Once outside, Ruger asks, "That was an interesting revelation— what do you think it means?"

"Honestly, I believe Valerie Vaughn had a talent for choosing the wrong guys. The other possibility is the CIA connection, but that may be a more far-fetched scenario. Before we wrap things up, I'd like to run everything by Kowalski."

* * *

Mary Kowalski greeted us with a smile. "C'mon in. Stan is up upstairs and in a good mood, but I'll let him tell you himself."

Even without the warmth of burning logs burning in the fireplace, Ruger selects a spot on the couch near the hearth. I take the other end.

Kowalski enters the room, appearing more chipper than on our last visit. For a man who may have been knocking at death's door over a month ago, he was now thinner and more fit-looking. Saying nothing, he shakes our hands and goes directly to his easy chair. "I have some good news. The doc gave me clearance to return to work. The only condition is to stay away from bad influences and donuts."

I ask, "Did your doctor put my name on your prescription?"

Even at my expense, we all enjoyed a good laugh.

"When are you coming back?" asks Ruger.

"Tomorrow."

I knew this day was going to come, but even knowing that, his pronouncement was still a surprise. "I'm glad to hear that, Stan. I plan on returning to New York, and pay my respects to Jessica by visiting her grave."

After a moment of silence, Stan asks, "What brings you two here, anyway"

"In a nutshell, we closed the case. Valerie Vaughn was captured, her boyfriend Max Bäcker was killed in the chase, the money stolen from the Madison Building went up in smoke after our police chase at Two Guns, and two hapless clowns got lucky locating the buried Wells Fargo loot."

Stan's eyes brighten. "Wow, that's quite a mouthful. Now, what information do you need from me?"

I pull out the envelope with Valerie Vaughn's ring inside and slide the ring onto the coffee table.

Kowalski leans over and inspects it. "This is a Nazi ring. How does it fit into the case?"

Ruger says, "We could have saved ourselves a trip and come directly here rather than stopping at the Barn Guys."

I ask, "Stan, do you have any idea why Valerie Vaughn might have been involved with this, Max Bäcker?"

"I'll tell you a story I heard many years ago about Nazis settling in the United States. At the war's end, the United States needed the cooperation of the Germans in their recovery. Additionally, former Nazis possessed organizational skills. General Patton needed them to run the displaced persons' camps. I think he recruited them against General Eisenhower's orders. Having served in those positions gave them credibility to seek admission into our country. And here is one more thought —the CIA actively sought the employment of ex-Nazis."

I ask, "So, Max Bäcker may have been nothing more than a former Nazi who just happened to hook up with Valerie Vaughn?"

"It may be as simple as that, but here's another tidbit. During my convalescence, I did a lot of reading. One of the most intriguing stories was about the resurgence of Nazi-hunters. You know, and this is pure speculation on my part after what you just told me, that Max Bäcker guy may have been on their hit list."

Chapter Seventy-Nine

Doug McGuire strolled into the Double Six Hotel amid clapping. He wore a new suit, tie and shoes—an ensemble straight out of the *Gentlemen's Quarterly*.

Phyllis Logan greets him with gushy approval. "Wow, don't you look snappy."

"Thanks," he says, looking a bit self-conscious.

Phyllis adjusts her blouse to reveal more cleavage. She says, "Sharon wants to see you. When you're done, I want to hear the whole story of your adventure. Maybe we could go out for dinner sometime?"

"Sure, ah ... maybe," he replies on his way into the back office.

Sharon Macfarlane rises from her desk and extends her hand to greet Doug with a smile and a handshake. "You're looking good. Are you here to work or dressed up for a night on the town?"

He sighs. "I'm here to work for now. Everything happened so quickly. I'm not sure what I want to do with my part of the treasure."

"I'm glad you're going to stay with us, at least for a while. Do you still want to stay on the night shift?"

"Yeah, I do."

* * *

Doug goes about his usual routine, feeling a bit more sure of himself and his newfound wealth. He thought of Ralph and his decision to quit the Flagstaff Sanitation Department. Actually, it turned out to be more of a forced retirement after he returned a bullet-scarred metal detector to the engineering department.

With the skiing season over, business at the hotel dropped slightly. He also enjoyed the respite, thinking about his new chick-magnet red Chevy Camaro. Once in a while, when no one was around, he would go out the front door and take a quick peek at it in the parking lot. *Life was good,* he thought.

A customer strolls up as Doug, relaxing at the ready behind the counter, greets the man.

"Good evening, sir. Checking in?"

"Yes, I am," he replies, looking at Doug's name tag with interest. "Are you the Doug McGuire who found the Wells Fargo treasure?"

"Well, yes, I am."

"This is indeed a fortunate coincidence," the man says gleefully.

"How so?" asks Doug.

"My name is Chester Bottomsworth. I am employed by the Wells Fargo Company. I came to Flagstaff to claim the property of said company. Of course, you will be handsomely rewarded for your troubles."

The news unnerves him and he shouts, "No, you can't take our treasure. We found it."

"That may be, young man, but it still is the property of Wells Fargo."

"We'll fight it," Doug insists.

"Don't be too hasty, Mister McGuire. You will need the resources of a good lawyer, and in the end, the state of Arizona will award us custody of our property."

"What is the reward amount?" Doug asks.

"We are prepared to pay you and your associate, a Mr. Ralph Tyler, thirty thousand dollars."

"Each?" asks Doug.

Bottomsworth laughs. "No. You will have to split that. And, of course, if you have used any of the assets, they will be deducted from the reward."

Chapter Eighty

"It feels good sitting behind my old desk again, " says Kowalski.

I laugh. "I know you're gonna miss me after I leave for New York."

"I don't think so. Detective Ruger is a lot better looking than you, and has better eating habits. So, what part of missing are you talking about?"

I reply, "My charming wit."

"Maybe so, " says Kowalski, "but at least you won't be tempting me with crullers anymore."

Not wanting to hear a lecture on food, I changed the subject. "By the way, I received some info on Max Bäcker from the Federal Immigration and Naturalization Department. It seems they were AWOL regarding tracking down former Nazis living among us. It turns out he was put on the list for deportation with possible charges against him in the German courts. So, I guess we helped facilitate his removal. "

Ruger walks in and places her briefcase on my desk. "Thanks for letting me use your desk, Detective Owens."

I reply, "On one condition."

"Which is?" she asks.

"That it is in as good of shape when I return."

After her boisterous laughter let up, she says, "It will be better than you left it."

"Well, I'm off to catch my plane. See ya." I wave goodbye.

Ruger follows me to the back door. "I hope you have a safe trip."

"I'm only going to be gone for a few weeks, so enjoy the peace and quiet."

Ruger hesitates. "Um, you said that you enjoyed baking babka."

"You were paying attention. Yes, I did."

"Maybe when you come back, you could treat me to some?"

I take her hand and say, "Of course. Babka is best when shared."

Epilogue

My readers may note that I have used real locations and names in some cases because hiding them would take away from the story. The stagecoach robbery of 1881 is real and the location of its treasure is still a mystery. According to official records, the gang traveled south to Two Guns (although it was not named that at the time), then moved west, passing just north of Flagstaff. The terrain was rough, so thy followed an old Indian trail to Veit Springs (unnamed at the time) the location of their hideout. After a shootout with the posse, the gold and silver wasn't located, making its location a mystery and the desire of many future would-be treasure hunters.

Acknowledgments

I am forever thankful for the cooperation of Henry Taylor and his wife Pamela "Sam" Green for the use of The Weatherford Hotel in this novel. By happy coincidence, the publishing of this novel coincides with Henry and Sam's 50 years of ownership of the Weatherford. What a historic accomplishment. Congratulations!

About the Author

Christopher Malinger lives with his wife, Eileen, in Central Florida. His works include *The Object of Desire*, which appeared in *Journeys VII*, an Anthology of Award-Winning Short Stories, published in 2014. Also, he was a winner of the Florida Writers Association's Adult Collection, Volume 7, *The Sweet Scent of Spring*, published in 2015. And again, in 2017, his short story, *Iggy*, was included in the 2017 Florida Writers Association's Adult Collection. In 2018 he was voted one of the top ten writers in the Florida Writers Association's Adult Collection, Volume 10, for his short story, *A Story Teller's Tale*. In 2019, the theme of the collection was *Writers at Work*, for which he won placement again for his short story, *Inspiration*. In 2020, his short story, *Jealousy*, was included in Volume 12 of the collection.

Other works include *Cat's Paw*, a fictional account of the bombing of British European Airlines Flight 284, published in 2016, and *Chinamans Bluff*, published in 2019. A collection of short stories, *Tales to Keep You Awake, The Back Roads of Terror*, and his novella, *The Wabele*, which won second place for general fiction in the 2017 annual Florida Writers Association Royal Palm Literary award contest. In 2019, *Scrubbed* received the Silver Award for the unpublished novella category.

His latest book, *Hit Send for Murder* was a Semi-finalist in the annual Florida Writers Association Royal Palm Literary award contest of 2024. In 2025, he received recognition from the *Writer's Digest* for his short story, *Moots, Toots, and Little Bit*.